The Thorn Trees

THE THORN TREES

by John McIntosh

HARCOURT, BRACE & WORLD, INC.   *New York*

For Gladys McIntosh

The Thorn Trees

The Thorn Trees

✹✹✹ Every day, an hour or so before sunset, when the heat began to drain out of the land a bit and the prickly pears changed color, the piccanins came from the kraal, sometimes twenty of them, and stood around the tennis court. The fence was rotten, and the piccanins silently chased wild balls that crashed through the gaps in the wire and tossed them back, always underhand, onto the court. Like the house, the court was falling to pieces. There were ridges of sand where a ball could bury itself, and the net was ragged. There were no lines.

"You serve," said Mr. Ferris.

"No—you. I began serving yesterday. It's your turn."

"It's too hot to argue. So call." He spun his racket.

"Rough," said Edna Ferris.

"Rough it is. So you serve, like I said in the first place."

They played until twilight, when bats scudded about and the spoonbill storks came home from the east on slow wings and Edna and Mr. Ferris could see through the crush of thorn trees the sparks from the cooking fires at the kraal. Then Edna collected all the frayed balls and put them in the basket, after which she unscrewed the big Ball's fruit jar and dropped into the cupped hands of each agitated piccanin a garish boiled sweet: one-and-six a pound from the Indian store at Gowani. The last to get his sweet was always Cyprian the albino.

The piccanins ran homeward, beginning to jabber when they reached the thorn trees, and Edna followed her father up the main path to the house. This path had a border of reddish bricks stuck in at a slant, separating it from dusty, stony flower beds. There was a network of paths in a geometrical pattern in the front garden. They continued to call it a garden although only weeds survived in it these days. Some of the paths had borders of baking-powder tins and others of bottles with their bottoms up. The few trees in the garden had bright trunks.

"I really must collect some lime from Peerbhay's," said Mr. Ferris, "and get one of the boys to paint on lines. Remind me. It's too much of a good thing, they do nothing all day long every day."

His khaki shirt clung to him. There was enough daylight left for Edna to see the sweat stain on his back, like a weird tree. His breath was short, and he took the steps up to the veranda one at a time, shuffling. At the bottom of the steps, on pedestals on either side, two stone lions lay, eternally sleeping. The one on the left had lost its head. Edna patted both the lions for good luck before she jumped up the steps.

The veranda was long and deep with a red concrete floor that was slippery when it had been polished. It was enclosed with a wire screen to keep out flies and other insects. The flies were a curse during the day, and at night, when the paraffin lamps burned, moths and beetles banged frantically against the veranda mesh to get in. In parts the wire had weakened, so some did manage to break through. They made for the smoky glass cylinders of the lamps and singed themselves, or burned themselves to death.

"We can bathe after dinner," said Mr. Ferris as he settled himself in a grass chair at one end of the veranda. His knees gave two sharp clicks. He sat with his knees wide apart and his stomach oozed over his black leather belt. The light from the lamp made his face full of pits and hollows. At the outer corner of each eye were smears of white matter. Edna wanted to wet the tip of her hanky and snick them out; but they would re-form soon enough. She did not mind doing anything like this because she intended to be a doctor and therefore she couldn't afford to be squeamish.

"So it's my turn to serve first tomorrow, no arguments," said Mr. Ferris.

"Don't you think we should stop tennis for a few months? I mean, it's bound to be a hot summer like they always are." Just the thought of the intenser heat to come made her feel tired.

Mr. Ferris glanced at his daughter. "I don't understand. Except when you were at the Convent, we've played tennis every evening since you were eleven, summer and winter." It was as if she had suggested that they should break with a tradition as old as the farm itself. "And tennis is the most social game there is, as you'll quickly learn when you go out into the world, which you will do one day soon. Very soon. You'll all leave me eventually, take my word for it. One by one you'll all leave me, my girlie included." He nodded gravely to himself, waiting for her to reply.

However, Edna did not want the conversation to go this way, so she remained silent for a while. She sat opposite her father, on the other side of the round table that wobbled and was covered with a crocheted cloth that had a fringe of orange beads like starlings' eyes. She sat strumming her fingers.

Edna had learned to watch what she said lately because Mr. Ferris was liable to take up an innocent remark in the wrong way and give it his own interpretation. It was thus wisest to keep to ground that was quite familiar.

At length the same old question that had been asked every evening for many years presented itself to Edna. "Go out digging today?" she said, knowing it was safe.

"I did. Over *there*," he answered, drawing out the last word to indicate a distance of some miles. "Near the windmill in Number Three Camp."

"Any luck?" she went on automatically.

"No luck whatsoever." Mr. Ferris leaned forward and tapped out his pipe into an ash tray made like a motorcar tire. The subject had been exhausted.

"Where's that good-for-nothing rascal, always late with

3

the drinks," Mr. Ferris said after an interval. Then, raising his voice, "Elias, shake a leg, man!"

"I am coming, master," replied a deep voice inside the house. "In half a tick."

There was a stack of magazines, the pages curled and the colors faded, under the table. Edna took one and flipped through it, wetting her index finger first. She looked at the pictures, which she knew by heart. The one on page thirty-six of this issue she liked best. It was an advertisement for a shaving cream, and she was in love, to a degree, with the man who stood there with his chest bulging out of his vest and the tattoo of a mermaid on the hand that held the razor an inch from his smiling, foaming face. She had been in love with him ever since the magazine had arrived in the post three months before. And she had put it in her mind that this was what her pen-friend in the United States of America looked like.

"Cross your legs or sit with your knees together like a proper lady, but not like that," said Mr. Ferris suddenly, making Edna start rather guiltily. She set down the magazine. "And your feet," her father continued. "They grow more like an elephant's every day. You really ought to wear shoes some of the time. In some ways you're a trial, Edna Ferris, that's no exaggeration. What exactly were you staring at in that book?"

She did not answer him but, to get herself out of embarrassment, countered with a question of her own. "Dad, I've been wondering: how does a person go about it if he wants to change his name?"

"*His* name?"

"Well, her name, then."

"You don't care for your name?" She offered him no reply, so Mr. Ferris went on, "It's my name and I'm proud of it, and your own mother took it and she was proud of it, too." He waved a hand over his shoulder, as he always did when he mentioned her mother, in the direction of the motseara trees near the earth dam, where the graveyard was and her mother and Grandpa Ferris lay buried; almost as if he wanted to beckon to her to come up and confirm what he had said. "Your own mother was a fine woman, let me tell you." He switched. "And what name did you happen to have in mind?"

His words had quickened, and Edna realized she had been foolish and off her guard to bring up this matter. "What name?" he repeated.

"Well, as a matter of fact—Marguerite de la Hunt," she said, giving emphasis to the name.

Mr. Ferris wriggled in his chair and knocked the stem of his pipe against his teeth. "Marguerite de la Hunt, what next. As far as I can see, you are spending too much time reading sloppy love stories in sloppy magazines instead of concentrating on your history and geography for your Matric. You used to go out shooting in the fresh air. Let me give you a word of advice, my girlie. . . ."

But Edna was saved from a lecture because at this moment Elias appeared with the drinks tray. One door led from the house onto the veranda, and he made his entrance through it. He was a tall, broad-shouldered Native who took dainty steps. He wore white, his chest gashed by the red of a head-waiter's sash. On his feet were takkies, tennis shoes cast off by Mr. Ferris which Elias cleaned every morning in the back yard, Oubaas the baboon watching him; and on his head was a cardboard sombrero with a now floppy brim that hid half his face. The sombrero, which was yellow with blue spots, was a leftover from a Christmas Day dinner.

"Oh my God, God Almighty," said Elias as he approached. "That Gloria, already she has burned the roasted guinea fowl that you have for supper." Although his knowledge of English was perfectly sound, he chose most times to speak in this stilted way. It was one of his affectations. Gloria was Elias's sister, the cook. Their father was Big Mac, who kept an eye on the neighboring property, a game ranch owned by the Davidsons in Johannesburg. Big Mac lived in the kraal. In Edna's memory, he had had nothing to do with his son. Once in a while Elias would take off his sombrero and point to a grayish scar on his head where no crispy hair grew, saying, "That's what my father done do with a chopper. When I was a little child." Before the sombrero had attracted him, he had worn a cap with "Mobiloil" printed on it, to hide the ugly mark.

"Cocktails!" said Elias in his incongruously gruff voice as he banged down the tray.

The tray had on it four glasses, a plain bottle and a fancy bottle, a jug of water, and a dish of salted peanuts. The plain bottle contained orange squash and the fancy one *mampoer.* This peach brandy Mr. Ferris bought in gallon jars from farmer friends in the Transvaal whenever he crossed the border while trekking cattle to stock sales. The drink was white, illegal, and potent.

Elias wound up the fancy bottle and inside, in a glass bubble, two ballroom dancers jerked round and round to a tinkly tune. They all watched and listened until the music ran out.

When the dance was over, Elias opened the bottle, and Edna's nostrils twitched as the musty scent of peaches reached them. The Native splashed the oily liquid lavishly into three of the glasses and added a dash of water.

"And the young madam's?" Mr. Ferris prompted him.

"Oh, excuse," said Elias in a mocking way. He unscrewed the top of the orange-squash bottle and poured Edna a drink.

"Cheers," said Mr. Ferris, taking up his glass.

"Cheers," echoed Elias, who swallowed his drink at one go, gulping. "Lovely," he said.

"That will be all for now, thank you, Elias."

"Very well, master. Bye-bye." He lifted the full glass that remained on the tray and glided into the house. However, he was back within a minute or so, carrying a green watering can. "Too much smoke in that kitchen." The can, dripping from its tiny holes, left a trail of water across the veranda. "Ever since the new madam went," said Elias, "these poor plants have been dying a slow death." In a corner of the stoep, against the wall, was a grandstand of ferns in silver tins. They were sick and lifeless, fatally diseased.

"Put that thing down at once!" said Edna. "I see to the ferns."

When Elias had gone, with a rather affronted look and his tongue clicking, she said, "I don't like him and I never have and I never will."

"Oh, Elias, he's a good sort really; makes me laugh, full of beans. It's your mother . . ." He pulled himself up in time. "The second Mrs. Ferris, I mean. It's she who spoiled him and taught him all his grand ways with red sashes and peanuts."

It was quite true that the second Mrs. Ferris had passed on a lot to Elias, nagging him, bullying him, and at the same time using great patience in her task of "refining" him. The same way she nagged and bullied and tried to "refine" me, thought Edna. Only she didn't succeed; like she didn't succeed with Gloria, the dumb sexy ox who burned everything at the kitchen stove and broke glasses if she so much as looked at them.

Elias had been Evadne Ferris's showpiece, serving vegetables from the left to the rare visitors to Sherwood Ranch and polishing the family silver every day in the back yard, watched by Oubaas, after he had cleaned his takkies. And it was the second Mrs. Ferris who had begun the custom of offering Elias a spot each evening and having him stand there and say "Cheers," like a trained monkey. Gloria had a drink, too, but in the kitchen, which was her place. Mrs. Ferris had pampered the servants in a way that had made the other farmers in the Territory laugh, but laugh with a sense of shock.

Mr. Ferris took a sip of his drink and rubbed his lips together. "Anyway, don't worry. Elias is going."

"Going?" said Edna. "Do you mean *leaving* us?"

At this point a bat got in through a hole in the gauze and, after bashing itself against the wall, began clawing in panic at the ferns. Edna picked up her racket and swiped at it. The bat gave one squeak and slid across the floor of the veranda. "It must be dead."

"Yes, leaving," said Mr. Ferris, who had not moved. "I forgot to tell you. Now they've got the vote and the Whites are clearing out and independence is rearing its ugly head, any one of them with some sort of education can get a nice fat government job. So Elias with his Standard Six is going to be assistant postmaster at Gowani. I can't pay him what he'll get there—so he's going. Like I said, one by one . . ."

"Oh, don't start that again. Please."

"Start what?"

There was a diversion. Gloria, coughing, plodded through from the house. There was something wrong with her chest. Her walk was a curious contrast to that of her brother. She was plumpish, but this could have been due to her age, which was eighteen, and the enormous amount of sugar she got through. Gloria wore shimmery dresses that had been discarded by Evadne Ferris.

Despite five years at the Mission school and all Mrs. Ferris's efforts, Gloria had picked up very little English. She stood at the perimeter of the lamplight, bashful, and said in Tswana, "My brother has drunk all my drink."

Patiently, Mr. Ferris uncorked the fancy bottle and poured five fingers of *mampoer* into the glass Gloria held out. There was a smell of peach brandy everywhere by now. The girl curtsied and went away, her tail shivering slightly. She left behind her a strong body smell.

"She's lying, of course," said Edna. "You know that. She drank the stuff herself. You spoil her, too. Next thing you know, Elias and Gloria will be sitting out here having sundowners with us."

Mr. Ferris stared at a point ahead of him for a moment or two before saying, "We see so few people. We should have some outside company; otherwise it's unhealthy. Maybe one day we'll take another holiday to the seaside?"

"Oh, you're always saying that." Exasperated, Edna got up. She walked to the end of the veranda and picked up the dead bat with her finger tips. She kicked open the gauze door and pitched the bat into the dark before the door banged closed.

When Edna returned to her chair, Mr. Ferris said, "It's exactly a year ago today that she left, do you realize that?"

Edna refused to take her cue. She sat with tight lips. There was no point adventuring into that territory. This had been proved time and again. It only led to her father's becoming broody; and he would talk about having premonitions of death. Yet every now and then, as if to hurt himself, he tried to bring up the matter: it was a month since she had gone, three months, half a year.

"Do you think she'll ever come back?"

"Dunno."

"You speak very badly, Edna. Say, 'I don't know.'"

"I do not know." And she wanted to add, "I don't really care, either."

"Actually, I don't think she will come back," said Mr. Ferris to himself. "Not after all this while." He turned his head, addressing Edna. "You never got on with your stepmother, girlie; we won't pretend. But, after all's said and done, I miss her."

Though there was no trace of self-pity in his tone, Edna sensed his intention. It was a kind of blackmail, that much she was aware of. He seemed at times to be weaving a web to trap her in, and she had to be watchful. In hinting to her that he was lonely, he laid a claim on her, his daughter, his only child, all he had left in the world, his girlie.

"You may not believe me, but I really do miss her."

Edna set her teeth. She would not yield, she would not be caught, as her mother had obviously been caught and, in a fashion, the second Mrs. Ferris. As soon as she was nineteen and had her Matriculation certificate, off she would go, leave this dusty land. She wouldn't desert him exactly. No, she'd come back for her holidays, nails painted and wearing stockings and stiletto shoes; and when she was a fully qualified doctor, God willing, she'd have a flat in the city and take dancing lessons and drive her own small car; and he could come and stay with her one month out of every year, one month, and she'd take him to cinema shows.

When her mind worked this way, taking a flight, Edna refused to stop to consider how Mr. Ferris might be or feel without her on Sherwood Ranch, because she knew that if she did there would be a big obstacle to her ever going. "You mustn't think about your father too much," Sister Clothilde of the Mission had said. "Otherwise . . . otherwise you'll become a wild thing, my dear, living there with nothing but cattle and flies. A wild thing."

At this image of herself, Edna quickly pasted her knees together. She dared not look down at her feet. Tomorrow she'd wear shoes, for sure. And she'd get some lemons from Peerbhay Brothers and start the treatment to soften her hands again. It was the second Mrs. Ferris who had said, "If you don't want me to teach you elocution and deportment, and wear shoes, you'll never be the lady your father expects."

"Marguerite de la Hunt."

"What did you say?" asked Mr. Ferris.

"A year since she left? It seems only yesterday."

"It seems much longer to me." Mr. Ferris stretched out for the *mampoer* bottle.

So it was a year ago that they had come back in the Ford truck, she and her father, barging through the gates without opening them, at two in the morning with the moon high, after having put Evadne Ferris on the train going south at Gowani Siding. It was when they reached home that night that Mr. Ferris, in a rage, kicked off the head of the stone lion. His big toenail turned black, and three weeks later the nail sloughed off. For three weeks he lay on his bed and never went out digging.

"Any luck?" said Edna, and as soon as she had spoken she knew she had already asked the question that evening. Thrown together as they were, they had a way of repeating themselves. All their conversations were confined within certain limits, and it was sometimes difficult to think of anything at all to say.

"I told you before—no luck."

"I wasn't listening. I forgot."

"Well, I'll tell you something else. It's there. *They're* there, rather—in Number Three Camp, somewhere near the windmill. I have a feeling."

Since she could remember, he'd had these feelings. But so far Grandpa Ferris's fortune lay hidden. Sister Clothilde said there was twenty thousand pounds or more out there somewhere in the veld, buried among the thorn trees and aloes, ten feet underground, sealed in milk cans.

Maybe the jackals had dug it all up and strewn it to the desert winds?

Mr. Ferris's head began going up and down. The lamplight turned the stuff in the corners of his eyes golden. "A year ago today," he said, "though last year the seventh was a Tuesday and today's Wednesday."

Evadne Ferris had gone before the previous summer had become cruel. She had said, "I cannot, I simply cannot any longer." She couldn't what? Stand the heat, when, outside, you had to scuttle from one stunted tree to another for the blob of shade they gave? At night the pillow was wet a minute after you had put your head on it. She had gone at two in the morning, waving from the orange strip of the train, standing in the corridor in electric light, her flowerpot hat nodding. Gone.

"I must go and wash my hands," said Edna, rising, "because I have touched vermin."

The bathroom was a dingy place. The plastic curtain with a design of tropical fish and seaweed, once fresh, was dun and tattered. The window ledge was littered with rusty razor blades and squeezed-out toothpaste tubes. The bath was lopsided. Its clawed feet stood on bricks, and one of the bricks had crumbled but nobody had bothered to replace it. Strange designs had been formed where the enamel of the bath had chipped. In the high corners of the room were clots of spiderwebs, and attached to the ceiling was a wasps' nest.

Edna scrubbed her hands with a piece of red soap that had a soda-water bottle top stuck on each side. The water, which came from a well, was brown and smelled of weeds. It was all right to use it for washing, but nobody in the Territory drank well water unless it had first been boiled. And boiling it took away all the taste.

The mirror, resting on top of a packing case, had a fork of lightning across it. Edna looked at herself in it for a few seconds, but the paraffin lamp was behind her, and her face in the glass was a blank. It was in front of this mirror that she had recently seen her father inspecting his body. There was a crack in the door, and she had watched through that. She saw him throw his shoulders back and try to pull in his belly.

Elias was waiting for her in the passage. Here a paraffin lamp hung on a wall bracket. His shadow fell on her. "Yes?" said Edna. "What do you want?"

Elias was grinning and swaying a little from his hips. His attitude stated that he knew he antagonized her. Since he had been a piccanin, he had offered to those around him not himself but a caricature of himself. "Oh mercy, that Gloria has burned the guinea fowl so badly, so now she must be cooking something else and therefore dinner will be delayed."

"Very well," said Edna, taking a step forward; but Elias was in her way, and he did not move. "I want to get past."

"Because we are going to be so late, will the young madam ask the master if we can have another cocktail?"

"Ask him yourself."

Mr. Ferris laughed and gave the servants a glass of *mampoer* each. Once Elias had disappeared with the drinks, his takkies squealing, Edna said, "What I don't like is the way he's always everywhere. When does he go?"

"At the end of the month, more's the pity," said Mr. Ferris. "He's faithful, you know. He's loyal, in his way." He seemed to be about to expand on this, when he changed his mind and said instead, "You haven't entered in today's scores."

Edna fetched the black address book from its drawer in the table which stood under the horns of the glass-eyed buffalo in the passage. Grandpa Ferris shot the buffalo when he was a young man. She wrote down the date and, "Archie Ferris beat Edna Ferris 6–4, 6–3."

Talk dried up, and they simply sat. Every now and then Mr. Ferris's hand moved to the bottle.

The meal was an hour later, just as the moon began to flip up above the thorn trees, making them lacy. "Dinner is served!" Elias called from inside the house, and they had to move from the veranda into the stuffy dining room, made hot by the large overhead lamp. The furniture in this room, all bought by Grandpa Ferris, was dark and heavy, and the floor boards creaked. On the table was a green velvet cloth with tassels that brushed the ground. The cloth was scarred with stains and cigarette burns. Once there had been dozens of crystal wine glasses with long stems, and now there were two left. Every night Elias laid them out, but there was never wine, except at Christmas, a sweet wine from the Cape.

Elias had had too much. It wasn't only that he giggled and sent out fumes of peaches. When he served Edna with mashed pumpkin and a fatty slab of steak (an ox had been slaughtered that week), he served her from the right, carrying the dishes with exaggerated care. Also, his sash was badly out of place, crinkled up under an armpit. In the kitchen, Gloria was singing. For pudding, there was stewed guavas out of a tin, in a sweet syrupy juice.

Mr. Ferris hummed to himself between mouthfuls.

"Want a walk?" he said when the meal was over, shoving back his chair. "The moon's bright, so we'd see any snakes in time. They're beginning to come out."

That was a sign of summer, the true summer from which Evadne Ferris had fled, the blistering days, when the snakes came out. The so-oopwha blowing endlessly from the west meant autumn; fewer flies meant winter; the straggly willow trees by the earth dam turning green, spring; and the snakes, summer.

"I have homework to do." She moved across to him and kissed him briefly on the forehead, above the clear line separating the white skin, kept white from the sun by his hat, from the toughened sunburned skin. Mr. Ferris threw out his hands and, catching her head lightly, drew her face to his lips. Edna pulled away as soon as she could and wiped the back of her hand across her mouth. She said, "I wonder if you'd ask Elias to remove the bucket in the morning. He won't listen to me and it's getting too full."

She retreated to her room, which was at the far end of the house, along another passage, whose coconut matting tickled her feet. She lighted her way with a torch. Once in the room, she struck a match and held it to the Handigas lamp. The mantle hissed like the sea and spread a white, glaring light. The Handigas lamp—it was filled once a month at the Indian store at Gowani—was a luxury, the only one in the house. Mr. Ferris had bought it so that Edna would not strain her eyes while she was studying.

Edna was pleased to be alone, in her room. Except for the "Palace," which she visited secretly, without her father's knowing, her room was her favorite place. There had been a time, when she was a child and a young girl, that Edna could not bear to be indoors. She had loved Sherwood Ranch. She had roamed the farm from dawn to sunset, on foot, on her bicycle, on horseback. She had assisted with the dipping; gone on treks with the cattle to stock sales or to the abattoir; helped put up fences and windmills; shot buck and guinea fowl. Once or twice, when she was on her own, she had even caught sight of the old witch in the heart of the veld. For years Edna had played with the Native children from the kraal, the piccanins and the little girls, Gloria among them, before Gloria went to the Mission school and then to work in the kitchen. And Edna could speak their language well.

Then, when Edna turned thirteen, her life changed. Evadne Ferris arrived on the farm and Edna was sent to the Convent in the south. She came home on holidays, but the farm was no longer the same to her. It had lost its appeal. She was happy at the Convent. However, her father took her out of it, for no reason she could at first see, after two years, when she had written her Junior Certificate.

She was back on Sherwood Ranch, and the place seemed to close in on her. The bleakness of the countryside with its flat horizons and dust devils and Afrikander cattle with humped, meaty backs and great twisted horns gradually began to appall her. She could no longer bear to be outside, exposed. She only felt secure when she was enclosed, in a house, a room, the cabin of the truck; or even the tennis court, because it had a fence of sorts surrounding it.

These days, now, when she happened to be in the veld,

she fancied she could at any moment be whipped off the face of the earth. It was different out there at night, however, when the darkness was a protection, like a blanket pulled over the head.

Edna's room did not look at all like the rooms she dreamed about. Her ideal was something out of an American magazine. That was how she saw her flat in Johannesburg when she was a fully qualified doctor. Meanwhile, she was content in a way with what she had. One wall held color calendar photographs and a few glossy film stars stuck on with drawing pins. There was a bookcase with her schoolbooks and notes, and on top of it was a vase that held artificial carnations. There was another vase, on the desk, with an artificial tiger lily in it, a gift from Sister Clothilde at the Mission. The flowers could do with a dusting. On the floor were a number of buckskin rugs, karosses, and on the bed was a Teddy bear wearing clothes and a bow tie. Above the head of the bed hung a picture of Jesus with a soft face and a silky beard, also a present from Sister Clothilde. The picture, awash with insipid colors, was in a frilly silver frame.

The room had one window, which looked out toward the graveyard with its low stone wall and garden gate. Over the two graves towered the motsearas. Beyond, the moon made silver paper of the puddle of water that lay in the deepest part of the dam.

Edna closed the curtains. Mrs. Ferris had run them up on her machine when she had first arrived on the farm and had been enthusiastic. The curtains featured little girls with curly hair, skipping, rolling hoops, and throwing balls about. Originally the colors had been bold, but the sun had sucked them out.

Tonight Edna chose to study history, which was her weakest subject because her head could hold no more than five dates at a time.

She went to school by correspondence course. Once a month a batch of Roneoed lectures from the College of Success arrived in the post, which Mr. Ferris collected every now and then at Gowani. At one stage, after she had been withdrawn from the Convent, there had been talk of her going to the Mission school, but only Blacks attended, and it was decided that Edna would be embarrassed, that it wouldn't do for a White girl to set such a precedent. So she studied at her desk in her room at home. Her father helped her as best he could with mathematics, but they both got terribly muddled. Once in a while Edna went to the Mission and sat on the stoep of the convent building with Sister Clothilde, who coached her in the setwork books. The convent had five nuns to it, and when Edna had finished her sessions with Sister Clothilde, the others came out of dark rooms, and they drank tea and ate little iced cakes with raisins in them. Sometimes Father O'Leary and Brother Martin joined them, the brother fresh-faced, perpetually smiling; and Father O'Leary telling a succession of jokes in an Irish accent Edna could never properly decipher, slapping his knee and bending backward and forward with laughter, which the nuns shared joyously.

The second Mrs. Ferris had also had a hand in Edna's education to start with, but here again her enthusiasm had not lasted, mainly because she could arouse no response in the girl. It was this woman, after all, who had wrung the necks of Edna's pet pouter pigeons.

So, chiefly, Edna was on her own, relying on the foolscap notes stapled in yellow covers from the college in Johannesburg. She learned whatever she could by heart, repeating sentences aloud, poring over the typewritten pages until the letters did jigs in front of her eyes.

Edna was determined to pass her Matriculation this time. It would be her third try. Toward the end of November, in under two months, when she went to the Mission, which was the examination center, and sat at a desk below the stage in the assembly hall, a little segregated from the others and brought a cup of tea halfway through each paper, she had made up her mind that she would pass. Her future depended on this, that shining future that would begin when she enrolled at the medical school. Though she had failed her Matric twice before, Edna did not doubt that she had the ability to study to be a doctor; and nobody had bothered to put her right about this. In fact nobody took Edna seriously with regard to it. She had no idea what training to be a doctor entailed. It was something to be faced when the time arrived. Meanwhile, there was the hurdle of her Matriculation.

In the distance, on the other side of the kraal, a jackal howled.

Edna studied an hour later than usual. By ten o'clock the sentences were dropping, rising, running into one another, so she stopped.

It was time to have a bath, one of the pleasures of the day. In the linen cupboard was a bottle of mauve bath salts done up with a mauve bow. Edna had been given these on her sixteenth birthday but so far she had not untied the bow or taken out the frosted glass stopper. However, every night she considered whether she should use the bath salts, and then would decide to save them for another, more important day.

She hung her dressing gown over the crack in the door, just in case. She had seen an eye there once, and when she had called out, the eye had gone.

Tadpoles spurted out of the tap with the brown water: some dead and withered, others plump as ticks, swimming desperately. She smacked at them, herding them to one end, from where she scooped them out with a tea strainer, which was kept in the bathroom for this purpose, and emptied them onto the floor. They struggled for a while in a few drops of water. Gloria would clean up the mess in the morning.

Edna had a plastic fish which floated at her feet. If she closed her eyes, she could imagine herself in the bathroom at the "Palace." She bathed in tepid water. Only in winter, for a month or so, was the bath water heated, in a big black cauldron, a missionary's pot, in the back yard, from where it was carried to the bathroom in paraffin tins. For the rest of the year they made do with water from the tap. Sometimes it was quite warm.

Edna lifted a foot and kicked the fish, making it spin.

The towel was threadbare and had holes in it. She dried herself quickly and put on her dressing gown.

17

On her way back to her room, Edna paused. She had heard an odd laugh coming from the kitchen. Funny things some-times went on in the house at night, and Edna had tried to train herself not to take too much notice of what happened after dark. The laugh was repeated—it was her father, guttural— and Gloria joined in with a shriek, which trailed away and ended in a coughing bout.

Then, for the third time, Mr. Ferris laughed, and made Edna prickle. She had never heard anything like it from him before. It wasn't a happy laugh by any means. There seemed to her to be some distress in it. She became curious and uncertain, so she switched off the torch and tiptoed to the kitchen door. She pushed it open a tiny bit with her foot and, closing one eye, peered in.

Mr. Ferris, Gloria, and Elias were seated untidily at the kitchen table with glasses and the bottle of *mampoer* in front of them. They appeared to be playing some kind of card game, but it was a disorderly game because a lot of cards lay scattered on the floor. Elias was opposite Edna but he could not see her because the brim of the sombrero hung over his eyes. Mr. Ferris and Gloria had their backs to her.

The laughter had stopped, cut off, almost as if Mr. Ferris might have sensed there was an onlooker. He raised an arm and slapped a card on the table, making some drink jump out of the glasses and causing the ballroom dancers to give one twirl. Then this same arm came down, went under the table, and Edna saw his fingers crawl up Gloria's leg. The Native girl did not stir. She sat stock-still, with a straight back, her head like a carving.

Elias thumped down a card and took Edna's attention away for a second. When she returned her eyes to the two nearest her, her father's hand had vanished up Gloria's dress. All of a sudden he lurched over her, put his mouth on her neck and bit her. Gloria squealed without alarm. However, he bit her again, fiercely, and Gloria jerked away and screamed. Then Mr. Ferris began laughing once more.

Edna's heart went tight and she hurried back to her room. Her mind raced and she could not fall asleep. Her ears were alert for any further noises from the kitchen, but there were no human sounds; only outside, the crickets and the tree frogs.

The pillow became hot and she turned it over a number of times. The Teddy bear was rough against her skin, so she pitched it off the bed. However, the idea of the toy lying on the floor worried her and in the end she leaned over and retrieved it. She clung to it for a while as if it were living and could comfort her.

She tried to rub off her mind what she had seen in the kitchen. She forced herself to think of the holiday she had once spent at the seaside. She pictured the cool green waves with the fish glinting in them when they were about to break, and she sent herself wandering among the rock pools.

Much later, people were outside the house. Edna heard the thud and shuffle of feet. She got up and lifted an edge of the curtain and looked out into the garden. The moon was bright.

Gloria, in the daytime so stodgy and ungraceful, was transformed. She was dancing like a goddess along the pathways between the beds of weeds, waving her arms, lifting her knees high and throwing back her head. She was naked.

Mr. Ferris skipped after her, trying to imitate her dance, seeming almost to be mocking her. Then the third member of the trio appeared: Elias stepped out of the heavy shadows at the side of the house and stood watching his sister and Mr. Ferris.

They were on the tennis court now, circling each other slowly. Edna had seen saddle-billed storks doing a mating dance like this.

Then Gloria broke into a run and Mr. Ferris chased her, his belly flopping over his leather belt. An attack of coughing stopped Gloria near the wall of the cemetery, and Mr. Ferris caught up with her. He grabbed Gloria's arms and twisted her round to face him. Her skin shone. He pulled her body gradually to him until they were merged, a blur against the motseara trees.

Elias shifted, moving back into the shadows. Edna let the curtain drop and she put her knuckles in her mouth and bit them until she had the clean taste of blood.

Two

✳✳✳ Breakfast in bed had been one of Evadne Ferris's innovations. It was served at six and consisted of Post Toasties, coffee, bread, and jam; and, if the fowls had been laying, a boiled egg.

There was the evidence of the bruises on Gloria's neck. Edna looked for them, hoping there wouldn't be any sign confirming what she knew. But when Gloria brought in breakfast on a tray, Edna sat up in bed, drawing the sheet to her throat, and saw them straight away, the bluish-purple marks on the girl's neck, like the start of a disease.

From that morning, Edna noticed a change in Gloria. The girl's meekness began to go and was replaced by what Edna took to be haughtiness. If Edna asked her to do anything, she made impatient clicks with her tongue. There was the business about the bucket. Elias said he was leaving and he wouldn't empty any more buckets. And when Edna told Gloria to do so, the girl refused; it wasn't her job; she emptied the bucket from Elias's and her lavatory, and that was enough. So Edna had no choice; she went out with a spade and a bottle of Jeyes's fluid. Twice a week she emptied the bucket in the bushes and covered its contents with sand, while Gloria sat in the kitchen rubbing a special cream into her face to turn it white.

Edna had seen her father and this girl dancing on the tennis court. She could never forget that. She searched his face for anything it might give away, looking for a clue there as to what his feelings might be. His face was the same; there was no mark left on it by that night.

There had been no change in his personality, either, that she could tell. And he continued his life as usual, leaving at daybreak in the truck with a packet of sandwiches and a bottle of tea, to go digging in Number Three Camp for Grandpa's treasure. When he got home, he called as he came up the steps, "Tennis, my girlie? It's your turn to start serving today." Or, "It's my turn today, girlie." After tennis they sat on the stoep, he throwing back *mampoer* and she drinking orange squash until Elias shouted from inside the house, "Dinner is served!" Once or twice her father even skirted again the subject of Evadne Ferris, in a low key, implying how much he missed her.

Edna said nothing. Her mind began to tell her that she should hate this man. He was a dreadful hypocrite. And yet she still wanted to get out of her grass chair and cross over to him and clean the corners of his eyes.

When the evening meal was over, she went straight to her room. One night she found herself talking to the Teddy bear. She was aware that this was a bad sign. "They're drinking and playing cards in the kitchen, I know," said Edna in a low voice. "And I don't care. I really don't. I really and truly don't care. They can do what they like because this time next year you and I won't be here." Then, in the grip of an abrupt rage, she snatched up the Teddy bear and flung it against the wall of the film stars. She went after it. She grasped it by the legs and banged its head on the desk until one of its eyes popped out on the end of a piece of wire.

The nighttime card-playing and drinking continued in the kitchen, but Edna did not return to spy through a chink in the door; and if she heard footsteps outside, she did not go to the window, but put the pillows over her head and thought of waves crashing on a white beach.

On Elias's last night at Sherwood Ranch, there was a farewell party that went on until dawn. They sang and shouted and laughed and ran around the house. Somebody threw a stone on the roof.

The next morning, Mr. Ferris did not go out digging. He lay on his bed. At noon he brought the truck, in fits and starts, to the front of the house, and Elias walked precisely down the steps, carrying a roped cardboard suitcase. Gloria was in messy tears. Mr. Ferris drove Elias to Gowani and his new job as assistant postmaster.

Once Elias had gone, Gloria moved into the house from the kia, the one-room tin shack she had shared in the back yard with her brother.

Edna saw the girl carrying in her belongings in a bundle balanced on her head, as the women in the kraal carried water from the well. Although Edna's astonishment soon gave way to outrage, she chose to say nothing, make no comment, because she did not trust herself to be coherent. She had no idea what she would say, how she would go about a confrontation with her father. For his part, too, Mr. Ferris said nothing. Gloria's coming to live in the house was an accomplished fact.

She took a room at the end of the house away from Edna, next to Mr. Ferris's—Evadne Ferris's old room. Edna told herself that it was simply a matter of time before the whole place was overrun with bugs.

Besides doing the cooking, Gloria now took over the waiting at table, in a haphazard manner. The month's ox had been slaughtered and eaten, and they were again on a diet of tinned Vienna sausages, and what vegetables the rocky field behind the outhouses yielded.

Edna set a limit to her silence on the matter. She was just waiting for the girl to start using the bath; then she really would tackle her father. But Gloria stuck to her custom of washing in the back yard, standing in an old zinc bath behind a screen of reeds near where the baboon was chained.

Gloria grew more and more lax. She stopped serving breakfast in bed and kept to her room until the afternoon, when she would come out to peel vegetables. She peeled vegetables lazily until sunset, singing all the while to herself. Edna had to see to her own room, and though no bugs appeared, dust and fluff balls collected everywhere and spiders scrambled across the walls. Dishes piled up in the sink, stuck together, luring the flies, until there were no more clean ones to be used for meals; only then did Gloria set about some washing up.

One afternoon, while Edna was studying in her room, she heard a loud crash, then the piano wires twanging. She hastened to the living room, which was only used when there were visitors, and when she had drawn the heavy velvet curtains to let in some light, she saw that the grand piano, which Grandpa Ferris had brought with him by ox wagon when he had come to settle in the Territory, had subsided through the floor boards. Though it had been out of use for many years, with mice and cockroaches nesting inside it, it had represented to Edna a link with the past, that past her father so frequently told her about, when the Ferris family had been well off and Sherwood Ranch a showplace. Now, here was the once beautiful piano looking drunken, gone through the floor, two of its legs broken, and snapped strings sticking out of its top like stubble.

When Edna told her father about the accident to the piano, he merely shrugged and said, "Must be the white ants. In any event, we aren't musical."

"Ag," said Edna, exasperated. "That isn't the point. Have you looked around you lately? We're living in a pigsty. And what about the bucket? The whole thing makes me sick."

That evening Edna came close to beating her father at tennis. She slammed each ball as hard as she could, so that the piccanins had a busy time flying about retrieving them. She had never beaten him. Mr. Ferris said that when she did, he'd give up tennis.

He won. At the end of the ritual two games, Edna was wet through. The spring—what little there had been of it—was dead and the summer had entrenched itself. The screeching chorus of Christmas beetles had begun weeks ago and would go on, relentlessly, for months. After a while your ears grew accustomed to the continuous daytime rasping, but at first the dry, scratchy singing was an irritation, as bad as a small insect trapped in the ear.

Edna was very conscious of outside sounds that butted in. She could tell, for instance, when a car was passing the farm gate three miles away, and she could hear the trains stopping and starting at Gowani Siding, even farther to the east. At night she would hear trains whistle far, far away, almost where the Capital was, it seemed. When the Davidsons flew over from Johannesburg for a few days' hunting on the game farm next door (it had once been part of Sherwood Ranch), her ears caught the drone of the plane before it was a silver speck in the sky.

Sounds round about Edna, however, made little impression and were taken for granted: the high nasal singing of the Natives in the kraal when they had kaffir beer or fresh meat; the jackals yowling and the Afrikander cattle complaining; and, except when they first struck up, the invisible beetles of summer.

Edna put down her glass of orange squash and straightened herself. "Visitors," she said. "There's somebody coming."

"I can't hear anything," said Mr. Ferris, hooking a hand behind his ear and peering through the fly screen.

"Listen," said Edna. "There's a car coming. You must be deaf." She ran into the house and brushed her hair twenty times and tied a ribbon in it. If there'd been more warning, she'd have taken off her jeans and khaki shirt and put on a dress, but she didn't want to miss the arrival. It was six months at least since anybody had come to call, and she wondered, with some excitement, who this could be.

When Edna returned to the veranda, the noise of the vehicle had increased as it strained along the sandy track through the mogonono bushes. Edna and her father stood on the front steps, gazing into the dark. At length a light appeared, one yellow eye that bobbed recklessly, hurling its beam onto the thorny bushes.

"It's not a car," said Edna. "Or else one of the headlamps has gone out."

A motor scooter came bouncing up the drive and its engine cut off. A figure wearing celluloid goggles sprang off it. "Hello, master! It's me!"

Edna recoiled. She had been expecting so much, hoping it would be some fresh face. That it was Elias who had arrived was a cruel disappointment.

Mr. Ferris, however, was delighted. He scurried out to meet his former servant and when they came onto the veranda, his arm was around Elias's shoulder, and he was talking into his face, asking him how he liked working for the new government and how much he had paid for the scooter.

"Secondhand from those Peerbhay buggers, but they are cheap crooks and it's no good for these roads. My back is already broken in two." Then Elias spotted Edna, who had squashed herself against the rack of ferns. "Why—good evening, young madam." He bowed low, fanning out his arms.

Edna went hot about the neck. She paused for as long as she could. "Good evening," she said in due course, turning her head away as she spoke. She had had the opportunity, however, of taking in how Elias was dressed. The sombrero had gone, and in its place he wore a porkpie hat. He had on a shiny suit a size too large even for him; cracked black shoes but no socks; a shirt but no tie. On his fingers were three glittering rings, the kind Edna had collected as a child from lucky-packets.

"You see," said Elias to her father, swaggering as he spoke, "I am a proper gent now. But already I have spent half my year's salary buying all these things from those crook Indians. God Almighty." He gave a booming laugh. "In any case, next weekend I am going up to the Capital on my buzz-bike to have a nice time. Would master like to come? Then we can go comfortably in the truck. There is a big dance at the Commercial Hotel and already I have begun to take dancing lessons through the post at great cost."

Edna thought, How times have changed. She knew the Commercial Hotel. She had been there with her father once or twice when he had gone to the Capital on business. It was a low-roofed shoe box of a building across from the railway station, where, until a couple of years ago, only Whites had sat on the wide veranda, drinking gin. The Commercial Hotel had been a sort of club for the civil servants and cattle farmers. And now Blacks were attending dances there. No wonder people were leaving the Territory, no wonder the old-timers sighed when they spoke of the past.

Mr. Ferris said, "Elias, Elias, I'm really pleased to see you! You must come more often. You're a tonic."

Edna was amazed to hear her father speak like this. She glared at him to show her disapproval. However, he did not appear to notice that she was put out.

Mr. Ferris said, "Oh, Edna, fetch another glass, there's a good girlie. And, while you're at it, ask Gloria to lay an extra place for dinner."

"What!" exclaimed Edna. "Do you mean . . . ?" But her message never reached her father because his attention and that of Elias were diverted at this moment by the appearance of Gloria herself.

"Elias!" The voices had attracted her to the door, and when she saw who was there, she swept across the veranda to her brother and skipped around him, clapping her hands. The two of them talked with great liveliness, while Mr. Ferris looked on, grinning emptily.

"I have a splitting headache and I think I'll go to bed," said Edna. Nobody heard her or, if they did, took any notice. So she left the three of them and headed for her room. The Teddy bear squinted at her.

She went without her dinner. Missing a meal was nothing really new. A crisis often occurred before or in the middle of one, to put an end to eating.

There were a few stale biscuits in the drawer of her desk and she chewed these. She couldn't study and she couldn't sleep. About midnight she heard the buzz-bike putter into life and then roar off. Mr. Ferris and Gloria stayed in the garden a while after waving good-bye to Elias. They were whispering.

Edna got up at dawn to catch her father before he left for Number Three Camp. She surprised him at the garage door when he went out to fetch the truck. She had worked herself up, but she kept herself on a rein. "I just want to say something . . ."

26

"Hello, my girlie, you're an early riser."

" . . . and that's that I am disgusted. I never ever thought you'd actually invite him to sit down at table with us. There's a lot been going on that I don't like. No, I don't like it at all." She wasn't going to mention Gloria specifically because the subject was too dangerous and she felt she could not yet cope with it. Nevertheless, he would know what she was getting at.

Mr. Ferris's eyes were bleary and his breath was strong. He had on his old school tie. He wore this tie whenever he went out digging because he believed it brought him luck. He had been to a church school in the Cape. In the dining room was a rugby team photograph and in the front row sat Archie Ferris at the age of eighteen, tall, thin, his hair close-cropped, his eyes clear. You would hardly recognize him today as the same person, thought Edna. And yet he was still youngish, just the other side of forty.

Mr. Ferris scratched himself and looked at his feet. He was wearing sandals and gray socks. "Try to see it this way, Edna," he said. "If we're going to remain in the Territory, we'll have to do our best to get on with them; now doesn't that make good sense? Perhaps I should make something else clear to you. That is that I regard Elias as a friend. A man needs a friend, you know. Who ever comes calling except the Roman? And he's only here when he's heard I've made a sale."

"Please stop scratching yourself," said Edna. "And listen to me for once. I for one am not staying here. My examinations start tomorrow . . ."

". . . and when I have my Matric and have turned nineteen, I am going to Johannesburg to be a doctor," Mr. Ferris completed the sentence for her, taking off her voice. He switched back to his own tone, speaking fast, roughly. "You are young, Edna, and you know very little and understand even less. Life isn't a fairy tale. Your heart isn't mature. How many times must I listen to that endless refrain of yours? *When* you have your Matric. Have you ever stopped to think where the money's coming from for you to study to be a doctor? Have you?" He shook a finger in her face and drew breath. "And as regards your Matric, I believe it's time you faced a bald truth. You may have been bright to get your Junior Certificate so young, but Matric's a different kettle of fish. Entirely different. I know. You haven't the necessary brains to be a doctor if you can fail your Matric twice running, even if you were under the average age." Edna noticed that the veins in his neck had swollen. "And—lastly—have you ever thought about me? What am I to do when you go? Sit on my own on the stoep in the evenings, eat on my own, play tennis on my own?" He was out of breath again and his face was marked with red blotches.

Edna found she had nothing to say, so she turned and hurried toward the house. The raised voices had brought Gloria to her window and she had poked her head out. Edna picked up a stone and flung it, but the girl drew back in time and the stone hit a pane and shattered it.

All right, if she couldn't be a doctor, she'd be a radiographer instead!

That afternoon, when Gloria emerged from her room, she did not set about peeling vegetables but sat in a grass chair on the veranda and flicked through the magazines.

For the first time in years, Mr. Ferris and Edna did not have their two sets of tennis.

Mr. Ferris drove Edna to the Mission for the first of her examinations. She wore a dress for the occasion, and a ribbon in her hair. They jolted along in silence. At length Mr. Ferris said, "Please forgive me about yesterday." He took a hand off the steering wheel and put it on one of hers. An impala frisked across the road in front of them. "You mean more to me than anybody."

Strangely, these words, spoken awkwardly, did not jar her; it did not strike her that there might be something false in them. "Me, too, my Dad. I'm sorry."

Edna began to cry. Mr. Ferris stopped the truck and comforted her clumsily. "Tears in the morning," he said, "mean laughter in the evening."

The Mission was five miles up the main road. Sister Clothilde was standing under a jacaranda tree near the assembly hall, waiting for Edna. She looked so cool and clean in her white habit, a snowbird come to rest in a fiery land. The nun pressed a holy card into Edna's hand. "I remembered you in my prayers." She never talked much, and when she did her speech was windy because of her chronic asthma. She carried on her a plastic bottle that she sprayed into her mouth whenever she struggled for air.

Girls in black gymsuits and young men in white shorts and shirts trooped into the hall, chattering nervously. Sister Clothilde led Edna to her desk below the stage, apart from the others. The din died away when Father O'Leary entered, carrying the question papers in long sealed brown envelopes with cellophane windows. When he slit open the envelopes, there was a loud sigh in the hall.

Edna closed her eyes and, though she was not a Catholic, said a "Hail Mary." Catholic prayers were the only ones she knew.

The first examination was English Grammar and Composition and it lasted three hours. Edna felt she had done quite well.

Mr. Ferris came to fetch her at noon. On the return journey, he said, simply letting the words loose as if they were of no consequence, "By the way, Gloria has moved back to her kia."

This news made Edna's heart jump with gratitude. She wanted to say something, to thank him, but her mind was jumbled.

Mr. Ferris filled in the silence. "I have also been to Gowani, to see if there was any post. And there was—and there's a book from the book club and a letter from your friend in America."

"Why, it's like Christmas Day!" said Edna. "Everything is going right." The "Toreador Song" came to her. "Look at that bird!" A bataleur eagle was soaring in the white sky, its wings motionless as it rose and fell, freewheeling on the air currents. The thorn trees hereabout had a hint of green; not like the ones on the farm that, the imagination said, a puff of breath or the touch of a finger could crumble, so dry were they after seven years of drought.

"Beware of such feelings, my girlie."

"But you must take all the happiness you can, surely? And I am feeling happy today!"

"I had a letter, too," said Mr. Ferris. "From Mrs. Ferris. She is never coming back. She wants a divorce."

"Oh," said Edna.

The truck turned right and passed through the stone gateway on to Sherwood Ranch. Another three miles and they were home.

The post lay on the table on the veranda: the book and the pen-friend's letter. Edna tore open the letter.

It consisted of two pages, and one of them was taken up by a drawing done in pencil, in detail.

The drawing gave Edna a nasty shock, instantly canceling her good mood. Her hands began to shake and she turned pale. Mr. Ferris had been putting the Ford away and now he plodded up the steps. Quickly, Edna stuck the letter in the pocket of her dress.

Mr. Ferris may have noticed the alteration in Edna but he made no comment. "Let's see what this month's book is," he said, slitting open the parcel with a penknife. There was an action picture on the cover. "Oh, good, an adventure story. We'll start reading it this afternoon."

Edna slipped away to her room and locked the letter in her suitcase.

After lunch, they began to read the book. At least it helped to take Edna's mind off the letter. They sat on the veranda. Mr. Ferris read a page, then tore it out and handed it to Edna. This was the way it had always been done. They rationed themselves to twenty pages a day, thus making their pleasure last longer. At the end of each reading session, Mr. Ferris locked what was left of the book in his tin trunk until the next day. In Evadne Ferris's time, she had on one occasion become so carried away by a love story that she had found the key somehow and stolen the book out of the trunk and finished reading it in the bathroom. When Mr. Ferris found out, there was an awful row.

The twenty pages were soon completed, and the afternoon

dragged along its course. Edna remained with her father because being on her own would mean she would have to confront the letter and she could not face that again for a while. They sat, she with a schoolbook and he staring out at the flat landscape.

At long last Mr. Ferris rose and said, "Time for tennis."

That night Edna had another look at the letter, more especially the drawing, a quick one. She threw it back into the suitcase as if it were a hot coal.

And she had pictured him as the man in the shaving-cream advertisement, somebody clean. He wasn't. How wrong she had been. He was foul, a beast, like Oubaas on his haunches at the end of his chain, scratching at his pink tube down there among the gray fur.

Still wide awake some hours later, Edna decided it was the heat that made her body feel like this. The roof creaked. She got out of her clammy bed—it was as if a fever were leaving her—and went outside. There, it was degrees cooler, and the air was water on her skin. There was no moon, but she had the torch, and she followed its weak beam as it led her to the graveyard. The gate gave a groan and the doves in the motsearas woke up and fussed. She shone the torch on the two headstones—the one of her mother's grave and the other of Grandpa Ferris's. The epitaphs, crudely chipped, read, "Safe in the arms of Jesus" and "Death, be not proud."

She shouldn't have. Coming to this two-grave cemetery always had a bad effect. Whatever it was she thought a visit might do for her never happened. It only got her to shed silly tears for people she had never known. Grandpa Ferris, the great man, he who had shaken hands with Rhodes and Jameson, had died long before she was born; and her mother had died when Edna was a few weeks old. Their lives could have little meaning for her. Yet the people Edna had not known or did not know sometimes meant more to her, in a way had more reality, than those she came into contact with. Her father and the others on the farm, those at the Mission, the oily-haired garlic-breathed Indians who ran the store at Gowani —they did not count as much as Lydia Ferris ("Called to her eternal rest" when she was twenty years old) or Arnold Ferris (1850–1936) or the people she would be meeting in Johannesburg next year, who existed but at this stage were unknown to her.

Edna pressed her cheek against her mother's grave. The stone was soothing. She released tears and tasted them, and with that salty, purging taste, the sex ghost flew out of her.

Perhaps she slept—she could not be sure. A cock was crowing near the kraal and she rose hastily, in alarm, and scratched her arm on a thistle. The place needed tending: there were weeds to be got rid of, and the fat obscene lizards that basked there in the day should be killed.

A figure was gliding away from the house, a darker blot on the night. Jerking in Edna's hand, the pale torch beam stabbed across the ground and sought the figure out, trapping it for an instant. Gloria's body gleamed. She was returning from the house to her kia. She had been in Mr. Ferris's bed.

Edna dropped the torch. "Liar, liar, liar!" she shouted into the sky. He had cheated her, her father.

Three

✳✳✳ The examinations were spread over three weeks.
Mr. Ferris drove Edna to and from the Mission. She sat
stiffly in the cabin of the truck, pressed against the door,
because she did not want him to touch her, not so much as
even brush his arm against her when he changed gear. Mr.
Ferris could not have guessed that he had begun to repel
his daughter. He whistled through his teeth as they drove. This
filed on her nerves to the extent that she wanted to shout
at him, "Stop, for God's sake stop whistling!" She checked
herself by digging her nails into her palms. She stopped herself, too—occasionally when she was on the very brink—
from accusing him outright about Gloria. This would have
served no purpose, as she saw it, because he would have
denied whatever she said. She understood this much about
her father by now: he was a deceiver. And yet she was incapable of damning him completely. He was, after all, her
father; and the element of sentiment could be strong in Edna.
There were even moments when she softened and wanted to
help him; but she could not tell what type of help it was
he needed, if any at all. They continued with their tennis.

On the last day of the examinations, at noon, Sister Clothilde gave a little party on the veranda of the convent building. There was beer for Mr. Ferris and Father O'Leary and
Brother Martin. The brother drank his thirstily and slopped
a lot on his trousers. The priest told long stories, showing
where the others should laugh by laughing himself, a sec-

ond ahead of them. Flies circled in a haze over the plate of iced cakes.

After a while, Sister Clothilde cut in on Father O'Leary. She raised her teacup and said, "I am sure you were successful this time, Edna, and I drink to your future. This is a big day in your life."

It was supposed to have been a big day; it should have been. But when it arrived at long last, it wasn't, really. There was no "Toreador Song."

There wasn't any change and she had been a fool to expect one. She should have learned by now—and she almost nineteen—that a certain day in the year, fixed in her mind beforehand as bound to be out of the ordinary, marked in advance on her desk calendar as the day from which "things would be different," turned out in the end to be the same as any other day; worse, in fact, because always on these particular days, before the sun had set, her expectations were dead, there was an awful flatness (even physical—in her stomach), and she was edged toward a void. Until another date—a day, a week, a month or longer ahead—was fixed upon and she went through the whole process again.

Edna could not prevent herself from putting up signposts ahead, which, when reached, she was sure would see a shift in the direction of her life. This never worked. The same old life went on. She felt she had lived a hundred years.

Yet when Sister Clothilde lifted her teacup and toasted the future, Edna had a rush of exhilaration. This, however, went almost instantly, and she found herself back in the same rut, the same faces watching her, hemmed in by mile after mile after mile of the same dusty thorn trees.

So another big day had fizzled. Anyway, perhaps she had learned a lesson at last, because, after the end of the examinations, Edna resisted pinpointing and forced herself not to think about the most important day of all: the day she would leave the Territory by train from Gowani Siding to start her real life in the real world. She avoided thinking about this day because she was aware that if it did not materialize, that would be a catastrophe, it really would. At the same time a voice insisted that the day had to come, it simply had to; there was no alternative.

For two weeks after the last examination, Edna did nothing except take her meals and play two sets of tennis in the evening. For the rest, she lay on her bed and stared at the ceiling. There was a wad of time to be got through until the results were published, and perhaps the least distressing way was to be as inert as possible. In due course, she knew from experience, the inaction would fade, and she would get up and resume a life of sorts.

This occurred when Mr. Ferris announced that he had a new plan. He told Edna that it had at last dawned on him that it was utterly useless, let alone ridiculous, to go on digging willy-nilly for the treasure with a pick and shovel. What he needed, quite simply, was earth-moving equipment, or else he'd spend the rest of his days, until he was under the motseara trees, in a fruitless search for the milk cans. Therefore, he said, though it was not the right season, he had decided to trek half the cattle that were left on the farm to the abattoir a hundred miles to the south and sell them; and with the proceeds buy earth-moving equipment. If his girlie didn't mind, he'd take the family silver along, too—but not the chandelier—and see if he could get a price for it down south. It all counted.

So cattle were rounded up, brought in from the various camps, and one dawn the herdsmen drove them, lowing bitterly, away from the pen near the house. The dust they raised shrouded the rising sun. Edna could hear the whips cracking like rifle shots for a long while.

Mr. Ferris set out the following day, in the Ford, to catch up with the trekkers. He would keep a check on their progress, sleeping in the truck at night, eating from the herdsmen's pot, and sometimes taking a turn with a whip himself. Along one side of the main road was a rough stony cattle corridor, separated from the road by a few strands of barbed wire, and the cattle would be driven along this, covering perhaps ten miles a day and being corralled at sundown in an enclosure made out of the branches of thorn trees. At night the herdsmen would light fires in case of a marauding lion.

Mr. Ferris would be away for some while. "Don't expect me back for a fortnight," he had said.

Edna listened until the rattling of the truck had faded. Her time of inactivity was over. She put on a pair of shoes and fetched the umbrella from its stand in the hall. Her father kept his supply of tobacco in a drawer of the teak sideboard, and she unlocked it and took out a tin.

A thermometer hung on the wall near the ferns on the stoep, and Edna went to read it. It said a hundred and nineteen degrees, but the thermometer was faulty. Edna subtracted twenty degrees to arrive at a more accurate figure. Ninety-nine in the shade. It was very hot. Summer had its claws on the land and there was no hope of rain. Once or twice lately clouds had banked in the east and lightning had flickered there, but it must have been quite a distance away, over the Transvaal, because no sound of thunder had reached Sherwood Ranch. Edna sometimes wondered if it would ever rain. It seemed to her that the drought had lasted all her life.

She unlocked the suitcase, put the tin of tobacco in it, opened the umbrella, picked up the suitcase, kicked open the fly-screen door and stepped out into the sunlight. It was so bright that she kept her eyes three-quarters closed.

The kraal was about a mile away and Edna headed for it. The sand burned through the soles of her shoes. Some piccanins spied her approaching and came out to meet her, no doubt hoping for boiled sweets. They hung about her like flies. A little apart from the rest was Cyprian the albino.

The only moving objects in the kraal were the fowls pecking at the ground and a Kaffir dog washing itself. No women were in sight—they were out in the fields or fetching water— and the men sat on their haunches, torpid, in the bands of shade cast by the eaves of the huts.

Big Mac's hut was the one with the pawpaw tree outside it. The tree had turretlike branches capped with slack leaves. Big Mac sat under it, like a buddha, gazing at his balloon belly. He let flies crawl across his eyes without brushing them away, although a cow's-tail fly whisk was at his feet. He did not stir when Edna's shadow fell across him. She planted herself in front of him and said, "Hello, Big Mac, and how are you? I wonder if I could have the keys of their house, please."

Slowly Big Mac lifted his eyes. They were filled with white marble chips. Many of the Natives suffered from trachoma. "Does the baas know?" he asked.

"My father's gone away for two weeks and, unless you tell him, he'll never know."

Edna opened the suitcase and offered him the tin of tobacco. He jerked a hand out as swiftly as a chameleon's tongue and grabbed it. Then, with a grunt, he heaved himself up and disappeared into his hut. He came out with the keys and gave them to Edna. She thanked him and went away, and Big Mac sank once more against the trunk of the pawpaw tree.

After a while, the piccanins gave up following Edna and fell back. Cyprian hung on a bit longer, and when she turned round to chase him away, he pretended to be picking prickly pears.

She walked rapidly in the direction of the "Palace," holding the umbrella low to throw the more shade about her. There was a stile over the fence dividing the two properties. Mr. Ferris had sold this land to Colonel and Mrs. Davidson after the foot-and-mouth disaster had wiped out nearly all his cattle. The Davidsons used it as a game ranch, a retreat from the city. They were never there in the summer, only flying over from Johannesburg for a week or a weekend now and then between the months of April and August. Sometimes they brought friends and there were parties.

When Mr. Ferris had owned the land, there had been nothing on it except a dipping tank and a scattering of windmills. The Davidsons had had the house built. They called it a hunting lodge. The Ferrises' name for it was the "Palace." It was a modern house, especially impressive inside, and it seemed to Edna a waste that it was occupied for a total of, say, only a month a year. She loved spending days there, but her father was against her doing this because he had come to dislike the Davidsons, saying that they were too rich and too arrogant and had cheated him in the sale. "Could you tell me what's wrong with your own home?" Edna liked visiting the "Palace" mainly because there she could sometimes enter a make-believe world, equivalent to the world of her childhood that used to come into being when she put on the fancy dresses from the trunk in the storeroom and paraded about the house.

It was not difficult getting the keys out of Big Mac by a little bribery. He was called the overseer of the game farm, but he had little to do, really, other than see that the house was swept out once a month and that the grass of the landing strip was cut and any ant-bear holes on it filled in. He was also supposed to keep an eye open for poachers, but he was lax about this and anybody could trespass on the farm when the Davidsons were not there and bag a buck or a guinea fowl. Father O'Leary was known to make use of the place; and Edna herself had often gone out with her .22 in the time before she gave up shooting.

There was a tendency in the Territory, when a house was put up, to place it closer to its neighbor than was necessary, as if to counteract the loneliness of the setting. A farmhouse all on its own was rare. They seemed to come together on the boundaries for company and comfort. Edna did not have too far to go to the "Palace."

Twigs cracked under her feet. She scared a herd of kudu and they careered off, tearing through the bushes, alarming and scattering the go-away birds.

The veld resettled itself into its stillness, and the Christmas beetles resumed their screeching. There was a slight, alien movement—not a mousebird, which she at first thought—in the corner of Edna's eye and she turned her head quickly to the right. The branches of a bush were stirring but there was no wind to make them do so. Maybe it was a leopard? There were still quite a few of them about. They splayed themselves on branches in the heat of the day, their tails in a coil, waiting for a buck to pass underneath. Edna strained her eyes. She could make out nothing.

She ran the last stretch. The stones of the patio were coals.

She reached the house and shoved the big key in the lock.

Going to get the keys from Big Mac and then crossing more of the veld had exposed Edna far too long to the open, and there was a tinge of fear in her. But as soon as she had let herself into the house she felt secure, and she got her breath back and her heart steadied itself. She let down the umbrella and kicked off her shoes.

In a short while the metamorphosis might begin. Gradually —if this day was like others at the "Palace"—she would change into another person: Marguerite de la Hunt.

She went round the darkened house in her bare feet, stirring up fluff balls on the floor. She knew her way, like a bat, without bumping into the furniture. At each window she adjusted the Venetian blinds slightly—just a touch to the cord so that a fraction of light shoved through the slats. Every room had these blinds, in pastel shades: living room, blue; dining room, gray; bedrooms, pink, green, and white. In the bathroom they were a bright yellow—daffodil yellow. There was a daffodil design on the tiles on the side of the bath. Edna turned on the tap of the basin and let the water crush down the drain the fish moths that were trying to scramble away. She washed her hands with scented soap.

Later she would take a bath. To go on with, a few dabs from the bottle of "Blue Grass" that stood on the glass shelf above the washbasin. Behind the ears. At the back of the wrists. "Slender, delicate wrists"—Edna made a note in her mind of the phrase. Surreptitiously, under the armpits, where her fingers touched prickly hairs that had pierced through the skin.

She hastily buttoned up her khaki shirt. The level of the "Blue Grass" bottle had gone down too much. She hadn't noticed this before. She'd have to be careful. She held the bottle under the tap and let an inch of water drip into it. She shook the contents, which became streaky like castor oil, screwed the cap on tightly and replaced the bottle. Next, she cleaned her teeth, choosing the pink toothbrush from the rack. First she rinsed the brush thoroughly, running her thumb along the bristles. There wasn't much paste left in the tube. She squeezed what she could out of it. She would have to order more.

Today, Edna decided, she would spend in the dining room. This room faced south and was cooler than the others. Somehow, the yellow-footed squirrels that nested in the ceiling never scampered above the dining room, so it was the quietest as well. Edna unlocked the pantry and fetched the fan. It worked off torch batteries. The batteries were virtually dead, and the blades of the fan revolved so slowly that Edna could see each one distinctly, like idling propellers. The air wasn't strong enough to stir the hairs on her arm when she held it right against the fan. She would have to buy more batteries, too, from Peerbhay Brothers.

Edna took a packet of XXX mints out of the pocket of her jeans, picked the waxy paper off the top, and placed a mint on her tongue. For a few seconds after she had crunched it up and swallowed the gritty pieces, her mouth was clean, but then it felt sticky and hot. She had better boil some drinking water now, on the gas stove, before she got down to anything. She left the water to cool in the kitchen.

As a rule slapdash, in this house Edna tried to be meticulous. She scrubbed with her handkerchief the part of the dining-room table directly in front of her. The pink handkerchief with a triangle of flowers embroidered in a corner (Evadne Ferris had left it behind) became blackened; and she, forgetful, dropped it to the floor and prodded it under the table with her toe, out of sight.

The key to the suitcase was tricky, but Edna knew the right pressure and the right angle to get it to work. She unlocked the suitcase and arranged the contents on the table, in a semicircle: a writing pad, two ball-point pens, the letter from America, and an exercise book that had been covered with brown paper. (On it Edna had pasted a picture of a bowl of roses which she had cut out of a magazine.)

Edna flipped open the writing pad, chewed the end of a ball-point pen for a while, and then wrote. Her handwriting was neat; she had always taken pains over it. "What to do today without fail— 1) Write indignant reply to him. 2) Write to new pen-friend, must be female. 3) Continue short story. 4) Read and listen to serious music simultaneously." At the bottom of the list, she signed herself, "Marguerite de la Hunt."

When she considered the matter, Edna had not had much luck with pen-friends. She had been writing to people in foreign countries since she was thirteen—it had been the fashion at the Convent—but not one of these friendships had lasted longer than a year. No romances had developed, either, though that wasn't strictly what she was looking for. Either Edna grew tired, or the people across the sea did; and the correspondence dwindled and petered out. She must have written and received hundreds of letters.

Never, however, had a letter contained what this one in front of her did. She had not looked at it since the day it had arrived; but now she felt she was ready to confront it again, and deal with it.

Edna took the letter out of its envelope. She smoothed down the paper on the table and studied the pencil drawing that filled the second page. In the empty house, Edna gasped.

Across the bottom he had printed, "INTERESTED?"

"Sis, for shame!" Edna spoke aloud and, surprised by the sound of her own voice, glanced over her shoulder, as though somebody else had come in without her knowing and had spoken. There was, of course, nobody there.

She should have destroyed the letter the very day she had received it, gone out into the bush behind the lavatory and made a fire of the onion paper and the envelope with its Statue of Liberty stamps. Instead, she had locked it in her suitcase.

Edna closed her eyes. The details of the drawing were sharp and clear. Fleetingly, she wondered if she was, after all, in some way interested. This thought made her shudder, and to chase it away she drew the writing pad to her, wiped her hands on her shirt, chose the ball-point pen with the black ink and wrote:

"With reference to your disgusting and obscene letter, I am too disgusted for words. I was not going to reply at all, but after weeks of serious consideration I have decided it is my duty to tell you what I think. What would your girl friend have to say if she knew? I have given the matter a good deal of serious consideration and all I can say is that I never want to hear another word from you and vice versa. What would my father say if he knew? All I can add is that I am bitterly disappointed in a citizen of America. A man should respect a woman, even if she is a perfect stranger. Do not bother to reply because I shall always be disgusted."

Edna folded the sheet and stuck it in an envelope, which she addressed and sealed. Then with the red ball-point she put a tick against, "Write indignant reply to him."

Licking the envelope had made her mouth tacky, so she went to the kitchen and poured herself a glass of water. It was warm, but she drank it all. She washed her hands at the sink and dried them.

When she returned to the dining room, the fan had died. She shook it, and the blades rotated an inch or two, then stopped. Exasperated, she popped two peppermints in her mouth and crushed and swallowed them. Immediately, she was thirsty again. But she couldn't go back to the kitchen after having been out of it for only half a minute. She would try to ignore her thirst, as she tried to ignore the heat, which had been increasing in the room.

The next item was a new pen-friend. There was a woman whose name had appeared year after year in the "Pen Pals" column of one of the magazines the Ferrises got. She would try her.

"My age," wrote Edna, "is thirty, and I am a happily married woman with three beautiful children, twin girls of six named Chantal and Charmaine and a baby boy named Wesley. Although I have no suitable photo to send to you at present, I hope to have one soon. In the meanwhile, I shall try to describe myself as best I can. I am five foot four inches in height and I weigh just over a hundred and ten pounds. I am blond (wavy hair) and my eyes are light blue."

Edna wiped her hands again and began a new paragraph.

"My husband, who has a degree in Agriculture from Edinburgh University, is a prosperous farmer, and we live on a cattle ranch of approximately one hundred thousand acres. My home is spacious and on the grounds we have an all-weather tennis court, a grotto, and an Olympic-size swimming pool with a filtration plant. As you may well guess, the majority of my time is spent rearing our three beautiful children. . . ."

All at once, Edna ripped the sheet off the writing pad, crumpled it up and tossed it in a corner of the dining room. She flopped across the table and bit her knuckles. Tears heated the backs of her eyes but they did not break through.

Boredom had to be prevented at all costs. "Be active, be on the go, be methodical," an article in a digest had advised. "Create your own interests."

Edna raised her face. Her hairline was damp and she knew that if she looked into a mirror now, she'd see a sight. She watched the blood spread back into her blue-and-white knuckles, and then she opened the exercise book with the roses on the brown paper cover.

A magazine had been running a short-story contest for more than a year. Every month it published the best entry and a prize of ten pounds went to the winner. Edna had been writing her story for seven months, on and off, but she could never get going because she was always crossing out and starting again.

"Nurse Fiona Hayward had slender, delicate wrists," she wrote. And stopped. She chewed the pen. She ate a peppermint. There was no inspiration in her today. She scored out what she had put down. "The doctor had firm, hairy wrists. 'Interested?' he inquired when they were alone in the duty-room, beckoning her to follow him behind the drugs cupboard. 'Yes, yes!' cried Fiona in a voice trembling with suppressed passion."

Abruptly, Edna snapped shut the book. What was in her mind could never be published.

Something crashed against the window, the Venetian blinds shook, and Edna jumped. Her thoughts plummeted back to their true setting. She looked toward the window and saw, beyond the blinds, a gray shape on the ledge.

It was Oubaas the baboon. He must have got loose. She went across to the window and called out, "Go home, Oubaas! Go away, you filthy beast!" The baboon hopped off the ledge and disappeared. A moment later she heard him clambering onto the roof.

Seeing she was up, she might as well fetch the record player and a book from the living room. This was her favorite room and because she liked it most, she used it sparingly, saving it for special occasions, for treats. The room was chiefly in blue and had many ornaments. There were big roomy blue armchairs and two low blue sofas. In a corner was a circular bar done in bamboo and four tall stools with tartan seats. On the wall behind the bar was the head of a black-maned lion. There were no pictures in the room, only four stuffed heads: the lion, a kudu bull, an eland, and a wart hog. The one thing Edna did not care for in the lounge was these animals. She imagined that their glass eyes followed her about.

Some squirrels charged across the ceiling and a wreath of motes floated down. Edna did not want to linger: she'd save the pleasures of the room for another morning. She hurried to the bookcase, which was near the bar, in a part of the room that was raised above the rest. The battery player and a stack of records were on top of the bookcase. Most of the records were cha-chas, and on the sleeves attractive people danced gaily against backgrounds of Manhattan, Paris, or Rio. But there were some classical ones, too. Edna went through the pile until she came across *Carmen*. She loved this opera. Whenever music sounded in her head, at heightened moments, moments that stood out on the plain of the long days and weeks and years, it was the "Toreador Song."

Edna tugged the *Carmen* box from the pile and in so doing knocked over a porcelain bird, which smashed on the floor. She scooped the pieces under the bookcase, blackening the side of her hand. The day wasn't going too well. There were bad omens. Maybe she should lock up, return the keys to Big Mac, and go home? No—not yet!

Edna felt she had already been in the room too long. She would be spoiling its effect for another time. She tucked the record box under her arm and went down on her knees to choose a book.

She closed the door of the lounge softly and returned to the dining room. The box had stuck to the skin of her underarm, and she peeled it away. Her sweat had made the cover crinkle in one patch. She took a record out, dusted off the floss with a corner of her shirt, and placed it on the player.

But the machine wouldn't work. It was flat. Edna tried getting the record to revolve by helping it with her index finger, but as soon as she took her finger off, it stopped.

Oubaas came down from the roof and settled on the window ledge. "Go away!" Edna shouted, and he vanished. (It must have been Oubaas who had made that bush stir.)

Taken singly, the day's irritations were not large, but the way they had piled up frustrated Edna.

She shoved the lid on the record player, carried it and *Carmen* back to the lounge, and slammed them down on the bookcase. Going back, in the passage, she caught a long splinter in her heel. She pulled most of it out with her fingers, but it broke off and the head remained lodged in her flesh. There was a tiny blob of blood. She couldn't be bothered to search for a needle and pick it out. She couldn't be bothered to wash her hands, though they were clammy again.

She opened the book, rested her chin on her palms and prepared to enjoy herself by being involved for a while in other people's lives. But she knew after five pages that the novel wasn't going to take her out of herself. It was boring and heavy.

Today, for the first time, this house had disappointed her. Always Edna had felt protected from boredom in the "Palace," shut away from the ugly landscape in an elegant place. There was so much to interest her and keep her busy, really. But today the house had let her down badly. It was almost as hostile as Sherwood Ranch. She wondered where the morning had begun to go wrong.

Yet she was not prepared to salvage the day by overthrowing her routine by having her cup of coffee or cold bath now. Those were reserved for later, in the afternoon. She would not upset the timetable. She would simply have to sit and wait, staring in front of her, letting the hours pass.

In the end, however, the house did not fail her. She had been in her dark mood for no more than a quarter of an hour when she recognized the signs of sleep. Sleep was a friend that had often rescued her lately. When it came, Edna was happy. Sleep—it was dreamless these days—took great chunks out of her life.

Her eyelids grew heavy and the ends of her fingers and toes numb. Her jaws cracked in a yawn. She drew herself out of the chair and made for the first bedroom. Sleep was coming fast. She wouldn't have time to close the blinds tight shut or take off her clothes, for fear of chasing sleep away.

The silk bedspread was cool. She let her mouth fall open. The instant before sleep took her, she was falling from a great height and her whole body jerked.

She slept for three hours, until after one o'clock. Oubaas, dancing on the scalding roof, woke her. Vaguely, she heard him scale down a drainpipe. He would probably find some shade under a marula tree and wait for her there, she thought.

Edna did not like waking up, and she clung as long as she could to the borders of sleep.

Her clothes were soggy, her mouth tasted vile, and the bedspread was crumpled and hot. It was in order now for her to have her bath and coffee.

From this part of the house, she had to pass through the lounge to reach the bathroom.

Somebody was there—slumped in one of the big blue armchairs.

At first Edna thought the gloomy light was playing a trick —as it had out in the veld at sundown, when she was younger, making her see strange figures and shapes. She continued for a few paces. But then she heard a deep, heavy sigh, and she drew herself up, going tense all over, and she stopped her breath and swallowed it. Her first instinct was to turn and run out of the house before she was discovered. But then she realized that whoever the person was, he was also an intruder, had no right to be there.

Heavy, dusty, round-toed shoes stuck out in front of him. Edna kept her eyes on them, expecting them to move.

She stood stock-still for perhaps two full minutes. After this her breathing became regular and she took a step forward, cautiously, ready to spring back. She brushed a strand of dark hair out of her eyes and whispered, "Who is it? Who are you?"

The man stirred slightly, and she half thought he was about to reply. But he was sound asleep, his head on his chest.

"What do you want?" Edna asked more loudly. There was no response—only a hand that lay palm upward across the arm of the chair gave a twitch—so she moved yet closer and, bringing her head down, gazed into the man's face.

It was Brother Martin from the Mission. This realization gave Edna a shock, and she moved back. Immediately she thought she had made a mistake. She couldn't have identified him correctly, so she had a second peep. It was the brother, and he was in a deep sleep.

Edna lowered herself onto the floor and squatted there, waiting for him to wake up. A shaft of light shifted onto his face, and she studied it and saw that in sleep he looked young, like a child, almost, with his rosy cheeks.

His hair was dark and healthy and trailed over his forehead. His eyelids, however, were smeared with blue and there were shadows under his eyes, like faint bruises. His lips were thin, slightly parted, and she could see a tooth shining. He had not shaved that day, and the stubble on his chin was thick. She wanted to put out a hand and stroke his hair.

Once or twice Brother Martin spoke in his sleep, a murmuring, but although Edna pricked up her ears, she could not unscramble the words.

For an hour or more, she kept a silent watch over the man. At one stage he cried out, as if in pain, and she had an impulse to go to him and cradle his head.

This was a curious, remote experience for her—watching a man sleep—but as time went on she began to feel contented, and pleased in a way, pleased that there was somebody to share the "Palace" with her, somebody toward whom she could be protective, somebody to keep watch over. It was like a game. She would not dare wake him up.

But at last Brother Martin broke through the heavy crust of sleep. His hand lifted off the arm of the chair and smeared itself over his face, tugging at the skin. His breathing became shallower.

He woke all at once, in a spasm, his eyes big with fright; and he pulled back into the chair with his knees lifted to his chin like a guard. An animal sound of fear came from him.

"It's all right," said Edna, rising quickly. "It's only me—Edna Ferris from Sherwood Ranch."

"Miss Ferris?" His voice hadn't found itself, was cotton wool. He cleared his throat and shook his head, and the sleep left his voice and it became normal. "I was sure you had left the house. It's the sun. I was in the bushes and I saw you come in and I imagined I saw you leave." His feet sought the floor again but the rest of his body remained pinned back in the chair. His hands were pinched together in his lap.

"It must have been Oubaas you saw."

"Oubaas?" His right eyebrow crept up.

"Our filthy stinking baboon. He was here. You must have seen Oubaas going home and thought it was me."

Brother Martin's lips pulled into a smile. He had even, wet, white teeth. His back came away from the chair and his hands loosened their grip on each other and moved to his knees. The cloth of his black trousers fell in folds between his legs, as if there was nothing there. Edna looked away.

"Why are you always smiling?" she asked abruptly, wanting to assert herself.

"Am I? I didn't know," he replied. "I have nothing to smile about."

She had been in his company quite often before, but now she noticed for the first time that he had a cast in his left eye. Later she would spit through her fingers because a squint person could be unlucky.

"Why are you here? I nearly died of fright."

His hands came together once more and he cracked his knuckles. "I have run away."

Edna saw a bird flying out of its cage. Her heart, too, rose when she heard his words, and she gazed at him, saying, "Run away?" as if he had done something altogether extraordinary.

"Yes, run away," Brother Martin answered, flatly. He was silent for a while, marshaling his words. When he spoke, expression was back in his voice. "I cannot serve God in a land where the trees are bleached bones and the flies are a plague. I have been here since I was twenty, from Ireland, the Emerald Isle, and that has been ten years. Ten times ten years! At the Mission, I was in charge of the farm. The chickens fell on their backs with their legs in the air and died. The cattle were poisoned from eating *tilp* and *slangkop*. The heat scorched the orange trees or diseases killed them. The sky has always been white to me, and the wind blows from the door of a furnace. In ten years your belief in God can shrivel, too."

Edna remembered him at the party, when he had sucked his beer as if for the power of life, and spilled half of it.

"I have been condemned before I die." A corner of his mouth was pulled down and his eyes were unblinking. His chin quivered. A dry sob came halfway up his throat, like dead leaves rustling.

All of a sudden Brother Martin pitched forward. He gripped Edna, taking her completely by surprise, his fingers stabbing into her. There was a smell about him like a baby, like milk.

Edna had never been held like this before. For a moment she was certain he had lost his senses. Then she had the impression that Brother Martin was clutching her in the way she sometimes clutched her Teddy bear. The tips of her breasts hardened. It seemed odd to her; something wasn't right. She was very uncomfortable. So, gently, as if she were handling a bird, she removed his arms; and he made a fist of one hand and coughed into it, embarrassed.

"Perhaps you would like to have a bath?"

"Miss Ferris?" The eyebrow was up.

"Please call me Edna. I said, would you like to have a cold bath? It's so hot, and there's a lovely bathroom."

"I'm a mess." There were blackjacks and burrs on his trousers, and tears in his white shirt where the devil-thorns had ripped at him. "I walked all night through the veld."

"But what about the leopards?"

"I saw nothing, not even a springhare, and all I heard was the ostriches, roaring like lions. I felt so free. I left after Benediction with the smell of incense in my nostrils. First I ran, then I walked. Only at dawn did I sleep, in a dry riverbed. I had to clear away the cattle droppings first."

"You bathe; it'll be lovely, I promise you. There are daffodils there." Edna rose and put out a hand. "Come. I'll make us coffee and there are Eet-Sum-More biscuits in the tin, though they might be stale. And if the batteries weren't all funny, I'd put on a record and play you *Carmen*."

She led him to the bathroom and left him there and went to the kitchen. The day had been given a definite purpose. She had escaped from her vacuum; she had been saved. She whistled under her breath the "Toreador Song." She lighted the Handigas stove. (It was fed from two big cylinders in the back yard that were filled once a year.) While she was waiting for the water to boil, Edna found a tray and a cloth and arranged the biscuits on a plate. She felt happy doing this. She put two heaped spoons of instant coffee into the cups, and carried the tray into the lounge. She crossed to the window and gave the Venetian blinds a pull, letting in more light.

The coffee began to grow cold, the unsweetened tinned milk in it forming oily patches. Eventually Brother Martin appeared, kneading his chin. The hunted look had gone out of his eyes. "I found a razor in the medicine chest," he said.

"Drink," said Edna. "And eat. You must be terribly hungry."

The biscuits went quickly.

The bath had washed the tiredness and strain out of the man and he looked fresh. He had brushed his clothes and pulled off the blackjacks. "Later," said Edna, "I'll mend

your shirt." He was offering her the plate. "No, thank you
—never between meals—except sweets. You eat them all,
don't be shy."

When the biscuits were finished, she fetched him more.
He chewed with his head turned a little away from her.

"You know," said Edna, carefully ordering her thoughts
into words, "I hope you don't mind my saying this, but I
always imagined that you holy people were always happy because you were so close to God, who would care for you
and look after you. Whenever I have been at the Mission, I've
rather envied you. Your lives seemed so complete and protected that nothing could bother you. You go to church so
many times a day, you do your chores, you eat, and you
sleep. And always the Almighty is there. It's peculiar. I have
believed in God since I can remember because all the Ferrises
have, being Christians. But my God is far away, in another
land." Edna found herself reddening. "Oh, I'm talking a lot
of nonsense, really. You mustn't take any notice of me."

"Go on, Miss Ferris. You aren't talking nonsense."

Edna shifted on the floor and toyed with the sugar bowl.
"Well, take Sister Clothilde, for instance. Despite her asthma,
she looks so good and calm that I feel God must be watching
over her all the time. So she's lucky, don't you agree, even
if she's got nothing, like dresses and so on I mean?"

"Poor Sister Clothilde. She is a fine woman and my friend.
She has tried in her way to help me. She came up to the
Territory from the coast thirty years ago because of that
asthma. They said the highveld air would be good for her.
Yet it chased after her and caught up with her. She lies awake
most nights, in pain, scarcely able to breathe. Her heart has
been affected. She'll die in this abandoned land, a tired sick
old woman, all alone. That's what's frightening me, one of
the reasons I must get out. I'm still young and, in spite of
that, death has become a terror to me. It's that I'm running
away from, I suppose. I've never lived, you see, had any
feelings. I was a pious altar boy, nothing more—and now
the God of my youth has left me."

"I'm sorry." It was a bit baffling, the way he spoke. Edna

put down the sugar bowl. "Is nobody in this world ever happy, I'd like to know?" she said.

This time his smile could have been real. "Maybe for a minute or two, at times. Not for long." Now he was staring at a point above her head.

"Oh. I see." Edna wanted to challenge Brother Martin's statement, saying that she for one would be happy once she was out of the Territory. She wanted to tell him that to her mind he was contradicting himself because it was clear that he was running away for this very purpose of looking for a happiness of some duration. Yet she had spotted some truth in his last words. Was Evadne Ferris any happier, she wondered, for having caught the 2:00 A.M. train from Gowani Siding to the Cape more than a year ago? Would she herself be when the examination results were out and her turn came? Edna shivered. She said, laughing, "Somebody just walked over my grave." She asked, "Where are you going?"

Brother Martin broke his gaze and settled his gray eyes on her. "To Durban. I'll hitchhike. I have a sister and her husband who emigrated there three years ago."

"That's nice." Edna rose with the tray. "Just put your cup on it and I'll go and do the washing up." At the door, she turned. "I'll help you, Brother Martin. I'll get you money and food and a blanket in case you have to sleep at the side of the road. But you should rest for a bit. Stay here for a few days until you are quite ready. Won't you do that?" She did not want to lose him so soon. A companion was precious to her.

Edna saw relief spread into Brother Martin's face and she realized that he must have had the idea that as soon as she had left the house she would get a message through to the Mission. He followed her into the kitchen.

"This is where the Davidsons live, isn't it?"

"You don't have to worry about them. They only come here in the winter."

"And you?" he asked, fingering a drying-up cloth. "Are you often here?"

"I come here when I can," Edna replied evenly. "I have

permission, of course. But my father doesn't like the idea. My Dad is a funny man, Brother Martin, and I'm rather worried about him."

"I don't know much about him. I don't know much about anybody. But I do know—we all know, that is—that you are the center of his life. Without you, he would be lost."

"Please don't say that! It's not true!" Edna rattled the cups and saucers in the sink. She wiped her hands on her jeans, and shunted the conversation away from her father. "Tonight, after dark, I'll bring you over supper when nobody's looking. And you can sleep on the bed in the pink room. I'll unlock the cupboard and get out the pink sheets."

She made up his bed, and after that they sat and talked for a long while under the eyes of the animals.

At last Edna made a move. "Don't go away," she said. "Promise me you'll be here when I come back."

The sun was dropping from the sky when she eventually left the "Palace," and she did not need the umbrella for shade. Oubaas loped out of a clump of bushes, showing his fangs in a grin, and followed her at a distance. When she had crossed the stile, she stopped and opened the suitcase. The baboon stopped, too, and looked for fleas.

Edna pulled out the letter from America. She tore it up into many tiny pieces and scattered them about her. Then she kicked sand over the shreds. The albino was watching her from behind a prickly pear bush. "Come here, Cyprian." She handed him the keys to give to Big Mac.

When Edna got back to Sherwood Ranch, she saw Gloria on the kitchen steps, peeling vegetables. Her legs were pushed out in front of her, and she had an enamel bowl on her lap.

"Put Oubaas on his chain," Edna told her. The Natives were the only ones who could handle the baboon.

Four

❊❊❊ That evening Father O'Leary came to the farm. Edna was taking an orange squash on her own on the veranda, out of habit, when she recognized the sound of the priest's Volkswagen. She moved into the house, to her room, because she did not want to see him. However, Gloria sought her out. There was a tap on the door. "The Oblates of Mary Immaculate wants you."

"Good evening, Edna," said Father O'Leary, shaking her hand. In his manliness, he always tried to crush your bones.

Father O'Leary looked tired and jowly. He was clearly in no mood for making jokes studded with his own laughter. There was concern in his faded eyes. No, thank you, he wouldn't sit down and have a spot. "I hear your father's away," the priest continued, in the brogue that Edna had difficulty in following. "We've had an upset at the Mission but it mustn't go any further than you, is that clearly understood? The fact is, Brother Martin has disappeared. Have you seen him, has he come this way by any chance?"

Edna met the priest's eyes and shook her head. "No, father, I haven't," she said, hoping that her words did not wobble.

Brother Martin was a new plaything tucked away out of everybody's sight in the "Palace" and she wasn't going to give him up so easily.

"It's a damned nuisance," said Father O'Leary. "It gives the Mission a bad name. We're not tyrants and we don't keep people in cells. I'll have to go to Gowani and ask there, and then the gossip will start." Edna accompanied him to the door of the Volkswagen. He turned to her. "I'll be much obliged, Edna, if you see Brother Martin or hear about him, if you'll let us know immediately."

That night, when Gloria had served the meal and left the house, Edna fixed up a basket of food and crossed to the "Palace." Brother Martin was waiting for her, expecting her. She heard the Venetian blinds rattling up and, when she stepped onto the patio, the French window opened. She flicked the torch across his face, causing him to blink and shield his eyes, before she switched it off. "It's you," he said in the dark, and he gave her a hand.

"I'll light some candles, not the gas lamp," said Edna. "We must be careful. Let the blinds down."

The flames struggled in the stale air and then started eating the wax. The candles threw lurching shadows against the walls. "I've brought you food," said Edna, unpacking the basket. "Bread and butter, see; eggs, tinned meat, real condensed milk for the coffee. We haven't slaughtered for weeks, so we're living off Vienna sausages again. They're quite tasty, really, if you don't get tired of them. Do you like jam?"

"Yes."

"I'll bring some tomorrow."

She cooked for him on the gas range, a mound of food, and she watched him as he ate it all at the kitchen table, every bit. "Scrape your plate with some bread; don't be shy."

They carried their coffee into the living room, and poured thick sweet condensed milk into it.

For Edna the evening had something of the recklessness and unreality of the midnight feasts they had had at the Convent.

She and Brother Martin sat on the floor, on the Persian rugs, and Edna remembered to keep her knees together. She had brushed her hair before coming over, too, and put two plastic clips in it decorated with pieces of glass to resemble diamonds. "If we blow out the candles," she said, "we can open the blinds and let some air in." The night gave enough light to the room to outline the furniture and themselves and the heads of the animals.

Brother Martin stretched himself out on his back with his hands behind his neck.

"It's peaceful here," he said. "I scarcely know you. It's funny, but I feel easy with you."

"Do you smoke?"

"No."

"It doesn't matter. If you did, I would have brought you some of my Dad's tobacco," said Edna. "Father O'Leary was there, looking for you."

Brother Martin jerked himself up, the tension that had recently left him clamping on him again. "They'll hunt me! In the end they'll find me and bring me back."

"Please, please." Edna leaned forward, her hands out. "I shouldn't have told you. Forget all about Father O'Leary and the Mission. You are safe here, I'll see to that. Tell me about when you were a little boy in Ireland and I'll tell you about when I went to the seaside on holiday."

Edna left at ten o'clock, when Brother Martin's head was drooping and his jaws opening with yawns. He saw her out through the French windows. She crossed the airstrip, the dry spruit, and then the stile. She ran back to Sherwood Ranch, dancing, jumping, swinging the empty basket. She hadn't run like this, feeling so free and abandoned, since she was a young girl and had been friendly with the veld. The torch beam was drunk. It did not matter, somehow, if a piccanin was spying on her through the bushes or a night adder was lying in her path.

For twelve days, Edna went to the "Palace" whenever she could, being careful not to make Gloria suspicious. As soon as Gloria retreated to her kia, Edna slipped out of the house, carrying the basket. The rows of tins of Vienna sausages on the pantry shelf were eaten into. However, Gloria did not notice. She sat in her kia for hours, trying to straighten her hair by various devices that came through the post. She also smeared her face with pot after pot of a special cream, but her color didn't change.

Mostly Edna went at night. But if she happened to get to the "Palace" in the daytime, Brother Martin read to her from *Wuthering Heights*. He had found the book, its pages yellowed and with silky spots from the remains of crushed moths, pushed away behind the others in the bookcase, against the wall. The wind that howled in the book and the strange creatures on those moors took Edna right out of herself, so that at times, in that close stuffy room, she shivered. "Go on, don't stop. One more chapter." And he would read until his voice was rusty.

At nighttime, after he had eaten, they talked. He told her, as she had asked him to, about his childhood; and she listened, captivated. When the idyll was over and he had gone, she could remember nothing; yet at the moment—the words came so beautifully, liltingly, from his lips—what he said was of the greatest interest to her. "I wish I had been born in a land of rain," she said once.

Edna told him things from her past, too: for instance, how she had cried for days when Evadne Ferris had wrung the necks of her pouter pigeons—the woman maintained they brought rats to the house—and had then served them up in a pie for dinner.

Slowly, Brother Martin revealed his nature to Edna, until she felt she had never known anybody so well as him. As the days passed, his right eyebrow ceased to go up and his nervous grinnings began to be cured.

Sometimes she wanted to kiss him, as a mother or a sister might. It would have been a pure kiss. There were glossy hairs in the depression at the bottom of his throat and under his shirt his chest was stocky—of this she was aware—and yet she could not have cut the face of the shaving man out of his advertisement and pasted a picture of Brother Martin in its place because he would never have fitted.

One night Edna brought over some *mampoer* in a Choat's Extract of Lettuce bottle. "It's a drink, peach brandy. My father likes it. Try some. I poured it out of his gallon jar."

He choked at first and spluttered—but he drank.

"When you were there," said Edna, "at the Mission, did you ever think of girls?"

"No." The flush on his cheeks was deeper than usual. "No —my troubles are not about girls."

"My father," Edna began. "My father . . ." she repeated,

hesitated, and stopped. She was about to tell Brother Martin about Gloria; she felt that she knew him well enough to tell him that. But all at once it didn't seem to have much importance. "No, nothing," said Edna when Brother Martin pressed her to go on.

The time went by in a kind of half dream. Edna was happy because she had a companion. She would have liked this association to last indefinitely, and whenever Brother Martin hinted that he had rested enough and was ready to go, that he should be moving southward in the direction of Durban, she grew agitated. "You can't go yet; please be reasonable. You must wait until my father is back from the abattoir and I can pinch some money for you."

Whenever Edna went to the bathroom at the "Palace," she splashed "Blue Grass" on herself. (Brother Martin had said he liked the scent.) Before long, the bottle was empty. Edna took it to the kitchen and pitched it into the Hygienette dustbin. The bin was stuffed with empty tins. She'd clear up later, removing all the evidence from the house, once Brother Martin had gone. And it was in this way that she unconsciously admitted to herself that he would in fact be going. As for the "Blue Grass," that created a problem, but an insignificant one at the moment. She wouldn't be able to replenish it from the shelves of the Indian store because the Peerbhays only stocked cheap stuff. She'd think of something. Later. It didn't matter now.

One afternoon, at sunset, Brother Martin finished reading *Wuthering Heights*. It was awful to think the story was over.

"I lingered round them," Brother Martin read, holding the book up and turning his back to the window so that the last of the light fell on the page, "under that benign sky; watched the moths fluttering among the heath and harebells, listened to the soft wind breathing through the grass, and wondered how anyone could ever imagine unquiet slumbers for the sleepers in that quiet earth." Gently, he closed the book.

"Is that all?" asked Edna after a long pause. "Is it all over?" She saw other losses to come.

"Don't cry. Please, Miss Ferris." Brother Martin was kneeling in front of her. "Dry your eyes, there's a good one."

"I'm not crying," said Edna, turning her head aside, surprised by his earnestness. "I never cry. Only rarely. I was thinking of my mother's grave and Grandpa Ferris's, that's all. There's no heath or harebells even, only blackjacks and prickly pears." She faced him directly. "My mother died when I was six weeks old."

He moved away from her, and she saw only the outline of his back. "Sister Clothilde told me," he said.

"It was she who took me to the Mission and looked after me, feeding me on tinned milk with a dropper."

"Don't think about the past and the dead; it only upsets you. Put them away."

"Take me with you!" said Edna, shocking herself with her own words. She had risen and stepped toward Brother Martin.

He held her hands in his cool ones and said, "I can't do that, you know. You realize that, Miss Ferris, don't you?"

Edna freed herself and brushed the hair out of her eyes. "Of course. I was being silly. I'm feeling all right now."

That night she took a spade and a rake from the outhouse and a lamp from the kitchen. She went to the graveyard and cleaned up the place.

The next day Mr. Ferris returned to Sherwood Ranch. He came at the wrong time, about noon, just as she was to set out for the "Palace" under the umbrella. When Edna heard the truck, she hurried to her room and hid the basket under the bed.

"Hello, my girlie, I'm back! Are you pleased to see your old scoundrel of a pa?" He hadn't shaved for days, and the hair on his face scratched her when he embraced her. His stomach was a pillow against her. "I've brought my girlie lovely presents."

His breath was stale and his eyes were raw. The white blobs in the corners were thicker than usual. "You've had a fine old time drinking as per usual, haven't you?" said Edna.

"Is that the sort of welcome I get?"

Edna saw in her mind's eye Brother Martin waiting for her in the "Palace," looking out between the slats of the Venetian blinds.

Gloria was on the front steps, bowing and smiling. "Hello, master, hello to you."

"Ah, here's my Gloria to greet me." Mr. Ferris reached onto the front seat of the truck and pulled out a parcel, which he tossed to Gloria. She caught it and ripped off the brown paper. Inside was a length of bright material, which Gloria unrolled and draped around her. She made her hips ripple, and Mr. Ferris gawked at her.

"And where's the famous earth-moving equipment you were going to buy?" said Edna. "Where's all this famous earth-moving equipment?"

Gloria left off her snaky movements and went into the house.

"Oh, yes," said Mr. Ferris, pinching the fowl's skin round his Adam's apple. "That. I'm afraid it's too expensive, exhorbitant. In fact . . ." He tried to push out a smile, but Edna's glare destroyed it. "In fact, I'll never be able to afford earth-moving equipment to find the fortune with until I've found the fortune itself. Ha. Prices are low at the abattoir at this time of year. Only twenty pounds a head, some fifteen. And I had to shoot ten cattle on the way because their hooves were cut to pieces."

"The silver?" Edna wasn't letting him loose.

"What silver?"

"Don't pretend you don't understand. Grandpa's silver that you took with you."

"Quite right, now you mention it. I'd forgotten. Yes, well —as a matter of fact, I sold it to the proprietor of the hotel, but the demand for family silver isn't what it used to be, either."

"Exactly as I thought," said Edna. She softened a bit. "Dad, when will you bring your head down out of the clouds and realize that you don't need earth-moving equipment because there's no sovereigns hidden out there in the bush in milk cans in any case? When are you going to put both your feet on the ground?"

"What do you mean—no sovereigns? Don't you dare say that!" He ground the toe of his sandal on a cigarette stub in the dust. For a week or so after a cattle sale, Mr. Ferris smoked Benson & Hedges.

"It's an illusion."

" 'Illusion'? Who's been teaching you such grand language?" Edna paced away, but he shot out a hand and took her by the arm. He drew her roughly toward him. Then his fingers came out of her flesh and smoothed themselves on her dented skin. "Why must we be at each other like this? We shouldn't bicker, girlie; we aren't husband and wife."

"I'm sorry." She threw up her hands. "A hundred times a year I tell you that I am sorry."

Mr. Ferris brightened, his chin lifting. "Don't you want to know what your present is?" He leaned over the side of the truck and drew back a tarpaulin. In a heap against the back of the cabin, under a plastic sheet, Edna saw a mass of blue with white trimmings.

"What on earth?"

"Can't you guess?" Mr. Ferris was beaming like a child. "Can't you? Ten guesses."

"I give up."

"Beach umbrellas," he said triumphantly.

"Beach umbrellas!"

"Why, yes. For the tea garden and restaurant you are going to run on the main road," Mr. Ferris said, patiently, as though he had told her of his plan many times before and she had forgotten. This was the first she had heard of it. "Twelve lovely imported beach umbrellas for the customers to sit under, like on the Continent." Mr. Ferris stripped off the plastic sheet and gazed at the precious umbrellas.

Edna laughed. "Everything else aside," she said, "tell me, tell me exactly who's going to come to a tea garden on the edges of the Kalahari?"

"You've got no enthusiasm. You put a dampener on everything."

"You seem to be forgetting something. When I have gone next year, what then? Who'll run the tea garden then?"

"It was just an idea," said Mr. Ferris, flatly. "Put it out of your mind." He pulled the sheet over the umbrellas as if he were covering a corpse. "I'll send them back on a goods train."

That day at lunch, Edna heard Gloria call her father by his Christian name for the first time. There was no mistaking it, even though the girl spoke in Tswana. "Archie," she said as she came through from the kitchen, "I have opened a tin of pineapples for you. All the Vienna sausages are finished, Archie, I don't know how. I went to find some and they are gone."

Edna got out of the house as soon as she could. Her father said he was going to have a lie-down, and Edna fetched the basket from under her bed and went away beneath the umbrella.

Before she reached the stile, she heard the airplane. Her ears picked out the sound in the stillness of the afternoon veld, and when her hearing had flashed this information to her brain, she was appalled.

The Davidsons were coming!

But they couldn't be, it was impossible, she argued with herself. They only came in the hunting season, during the winter, and this was the middle of December. It was a charter plane going to the swamps.

She dropped the umbrella and basket and, shading her eyes against the glare, raked the horizon. Some gray louries, skimming the tops of the thorn trees in sluggish flight, deflected her attention for a moment. "One for sorrow, two for joy, three for a letter, four for a boy." The go-away birds melted out of sight.

Then Edna's eyes caught the fragment of mirror in the sky and she knew. She knew without a doubt that the Davidsons were coming. Her little world, new and fresh, hardly two weeks old, began to disintegrate.

The landing strip lay between her and the "Palace," to her right. She ran there, jumping down one bank of the dried-up spruit and up the other. She ran like a hare, springing across the hot patches of sand. When at length she crouched behind an anthill on the margin of the landing strip, the noises of the bush had been overthrown by a steady drone. The piece of silver, a coin in the sky now, was spinning downward.

The sound of the plane had alerted Big Mac, too, disturbed his days of inertia under the pawpaw tree. Edna saw him waddling toward the "Palace," his head a few inches in front of his body, like a tortoise. He must be wondering, thought Edna, as she herself was wondering, about the reason for this sudden and unexpected visit.

Edna was on the verge of panic. There was no way of getting to the "Palace" and warning Brother Martin. She could only hope that he had heard the plane and had had the sense to get out.

The shadow of the plane slapped against Edna as it circled the landing strip and, a reflex, she flattened herself on the ground. Ants nipped her. Her ears were bursting with the din of the plane's engine. It seemed to shriek and whine and curse and threaten. By now hundreds of birds had been scared out of the bushes, but their cries were soundless to Edna. Two meerkats raced off the landing strip, streaks of orange, as the plane whirred in, its wings tipping, then leveling. Edna glimpsed a blur of faces behind glass and she felt the earth shiver slightly as the wheels of the plane struck the ground. It bounced wildly, and Edna, peeping over the top of the anthill, imagined that it would turn over; but Captain Davidson—he had flown bombers in the war—reined the plane in. It stopped, and the engine cut off. For a moment there was the familiar stillness, as if there had been no plane, no interruption at all. She was going to the "Palace," and he would be waiting for her there, behind the Venetian blinds. A host of widow birds resettled themselves on euphorbia trees. Edna brushed ants off her.

There was city laughter and the flash of bright holiday clothes. Two men jumped out of the plane and lifted down two women. Edna recognized Mrs. Davidson straight away because of her red hair and the gold slacks she always wore when she visited the game ranch. Captain Davidson she knew, too, from the way he stood—upright, as if he were in a brace—and from the blot on his face which told her where his heavy moustache was. The other two she could not recognize.

Their laughter carried clearly across the landing strip to Edna: Mrs. Davidson's shrill; her husband's cannoning; the strangers laughing in attendance. Captain Davidson hauled suitcases and boxes of provisions out of the plane, and the four interlopers, the thieves of Edna's day, began to stroll across the dry crackling grass to the house. Their laughter trailed behind them. Edna wished she had the power to send them away again. Once at a film show at the Convent there had been a very funny comedy in which the characters had run backward at great speed into old cars with canvas tops, and the cars themselves had then shot off backward. She would have liked to see the four people and the plane do just that.

They were nearing the edge of the landing strip and Big Mac was coming to meet them, his arms raised, shaking his head.

Edna fled back to Sherwood Ranch and sat in her room. She held the Teddy bear in her lap and nursed it. What had been between Brother Martin and her was over now. She should have known that it could never have lasted: he her toy brother hidden away in a "hunting lodge" belonging to city people; it was too unreal. If he had escaped from the house—and there was no point in thinking otherwise— he would need help. She had promised him food, money, a blanket for his journey.

She remembered the basket and the umbrella abandoned by her near the stile and she went out to recover them. The Davidsons must have brought fresh batteries for the record player because she heard a cha-cha coming from the "Palace."

Brother Martin would be in the vicinity, lying low in a donga among the bushes. "Are you there?" she called. "It's me—Edna." There was no answer and, at the house, the cha-cha came to an end. Edna whispered, "I'll come back tonight. With the things. Wait for me wherever you are."

The blanket was easy, taken from the cupboard in the

bathroom. But slipping the money out of her father's sports jacket would be trickier, would need timing. At the moment he was still in his room, dozing, so she couldn't do anything. She would have to wait.

To get through some of the hours until darkness, she decided to give the trees in the garden a new coat of paint. She put on a hat and fetched brushes and pots from the storeroom. She splashed the trunks with green and blue and yellow. From a distance, Cyprian watched her. Painting the trees had been one of Evadne Ferris's ideas: she said it gave the place a touch of much-needed color. Edna worked feverishly.

Mr. Ferris came up behind her. "Tennis! Time for tennis." He had dashed water on his puffy face and combed his hair, but the heaviness of a summer afternoon's sleep remained on him. The flesh of his cheeks was spongy. He looked old. "All the piccanins are lined up, so go and get the sweets and put on your takkies."

"You gave me a fright, creeping up on me like that. Do you know that the Davidsons are here? Did you hear the plane?"

"Don't mention the Davidsons to me," said Mr. Ferris, stiffly. "My, the trees are looking lovely."

"I'll be with you in a minute," said Edna.

She ran into the house and along the passage with its prickly coir matting. His sports jacket hung in the wardrobe in his room, on a wire hanger, the solitary piece of clothing there. The mothballs on the bottom of the wardrobe rolled about when she tugged open the doors. Her fingers sought the money. There was a wad of notes, sticky and furry to the touch: not enough for earth-moving equipment but enough for them to live on for the next few months. Edna sloughed off ten pounds. Mr. Ferris wasn't likely to miss it; he never kept a check on money. Ten pounds would see Brother Martin into South Africa, to Durban, to his sister and his new life. Another pound, just in case, a *bonsella;* and from the pile on the dressing table, a handful of silver. She got out of the room as quickly as possible.

Mr. Ferris beat Edna 8–6, 7–5. The piccanins received their

boiled sweets and returned to the kraal. One of them trundled a contraption with wheels made out of wire.

"You're going to win. One day soon you'll beat me," said Mr. Ferris. "What a wailing and gnashing of teeth there will be then. It will be a sign."

Edna entered up the date and the scores in the black book on the hall stand.

"Archie." Gloria slouched onto the veranda, looking fixedly at Edna. "Archie," she said, "I have brought you your drinks and come for my *mampoer*." She put the tray on the grass table and wound up the fancy bottle. The ballroom dancers did their turn.

Her calling him "Archie" now, this was deliberate. Gloria continued to stare at Edna, as if defying her to say something. Edna, however, remained silent and refused to meet Gloria's challenge. She merely ran her eyes over the girl and away. Redness showed on Mr. Ferris's face as he filled a glass with *mampoer*.

Gloria stood her ground, and when Mr. Ferris handed her her drink, she curtsied and said, "Thank you, Archie."

The girl had scored a victory at the expense of Edna. Edna was conscious of this and she was also aware that something was expected of her—some wild, ranting scene, perhaps. But she was determined not to supply it. She said nothing and she did not move.

Gloria was waiting, and there was a long, painful pause. Mr. Ferris leaned forward and took a cigarette out of the gold box. He let the match burn almost to his finger tips before he lighted the cigarette. The charred stick fell onto the floor. Edna, for something to do, to unfreeze herself, bent down and picked it up. When she straightened up, she felt Gloria's eyes still on her.

At long last Mr. Ferris said, "That will do, Gloria, thank you. You'd better be off to the kitchen before the dinner goes up in flames."

This scene did not have the effect on Edna it ordinarily would because half her mind was occupied with Brother Martin. She was longing now to find him and she wished the conventional evening with her father would soon be over so that she could go out into the dark to meet him. He was waiting for her in the bushes near the "Palace." She was certain of this.

She wanted so much to see Brother Martin again. Their brief friendship, she felt, would be incomplete if she didn't. There was something missing. Although their two weeks together had been a gift from time, she yearned for, she desired . . . What was it that she wanted so keenly? Edna asked herself. An autograph, a keepsake, a snippet of hair? Something more from time, an extenuation, another week? No, that might spoil everything.

"I'm sorry, girlie," said Mr. Ferris, "about that." He was looking at the tips of his sandals. His little finger dug into an ear and jigged.

"What?" said Edna, her head rising.

"About . . . Gloria," he said, tentatively.

She sipped her orange squash, and drew up her shoulders. "Oh, I told you, my Dad, I told you before that they will take over the house. I prophesied it. In a year, Gloria and her brother will be installed here and you will be in the kia."

Mr. Ferris took hold of the arms of his grass chair. "I am a lonely man, Edna. I don't think you've fully realized that. I love you." He looked inquiringly at Edna, but she did not interrupt him. He continued, speaking under pressure, "Yes, I do love you, and one day—don't laugh at me—I really am going to find your Grandpa's money and make you a happy girl." His eyes wandered away from her. "Try, if you can, to understand: that other thing is lust, not love. Sometimes at night I wake up, in a sweat of fear, because I have dreamed that death is waiting for me. And I am only forty-two. But when . . . when there is somebody in my bed, I feel safe for a while, there is some life left for me."

"Stop!" said Edna. She put her hands on her ears. "Stop. I don't want to hear any more."

Elias on his buzz-bike delivered her. Its yellow eye appeared among the thorn trees.

Edna stood up. "It's him. But he only comes on Wednesdays."

"Don't be cross—I invited him." Mr. Ferris looked guilty. He consulted his watch. "But only for after dinner. He's early. You see, it's like this, actually: I've had a good idea and that's that I should teach you all how to play auction bridge, something more advanced than rummy, so that we can pass many pleasant social evenings together, you included."

"I hate cards." Edna was badly confused. "They keep dropping out of my hands."

"Hello, all and sundry!" came Elias's deep voice when the engine of the buzz-bike had died and its eye gone blind. He pranced up the steps and sailed through the fly-screen door. (Its squeaking was growing worse; nobody bothered to use the oilcan.) Elias pirouetted. "Do you like my new suit? It cost me a complete whole month's fortune of a salary at those robbers the Indians. Plus shoes and my new hat to hide my whatnot." The suit was shiny with Lurex threads. He brushed the legs of the trousers vigorously. "God Almighty, these damned roads are too much dust. One day they will all be tarred when I am in heaven."

"Can't you get *me* a job in the post office?" said Mr. Ferris.

Elias went on with his act. "Easy as winking. Tell me when." He flicked at his shoes with a hanky, not the one from his breast pocket, but a spare. "Also, I have filled in a coupon for a course of lessons on records to improve my English and then I can be transferred to the Capital where the high-and-mighties are. I must first buy a gramophone to play them on. The cost of living, oh my word."

Edna began to move along the wall, but Elias spotted her. "Ah, the young madam is here! I did not see before."

"Don't bow and scrape!" she said sharply. "I'm sorry," she went on in her normal voice. "I have a headache. I'm going to bed."

"No supper?" said Mr. Ferris. "We can send in a tray?"

"I'm not hungry."

Edna threw herself on her bed. Her father had virtually

admitted to her what was going on with Gloria. She tried to chase away the things he had said, but they persisted in her mind.

Lust. He had spoken of that.

Edna turned onto her back and the Teddy bear squeaked. It was almost as if the bear had said, "Fucking."

Edna put her head under the pillow. "Fuck you!" her father had shouted at Evadne Ferris, one wild night in the house when they had thought Edna was asleep. But she had heard everything through the door of her bedroom. "Fuck you, you whore!"

The sex bogey trapped Edna, and she saw, muddled up together, Oubaas intrigued by his pink tube and the scale diagram the pen-friend had sent.

If only the clean man in the advertisement could come by magic into her life and carry her away.

As a child she had had a storybook about a boy who had been given a secret liquid by a wizard, which, when it was poured onto pictures of food, turned the food into the real thing—chocolate cakes, ice cream, puddings. For years she had played a game, wondering how she would use the liquid should a bottle of it come into her hands. Then she had passed into her teens and forgotten it. She recalled the story now, however, and she imagined scattering a few precious drops on the man with the shaving cream and she pictured his coming to life, rising off the page, a bit wet to begin with but quickly drying, and taking her in his arms.

But what, she thought with horror, what if he turned out to be a miniature man with the same proportions he had in the advertisement?

A dark part of her mind gave a solution. In that case, she would keep him locked in her desk and would let him out when she wanted to and play with him as if he were a doll. She would be cruel to him if she felt like it: she would twist his arms and pull out the hairs on his chest. She would throw him into the air and let him try to land on his feet, like a cat. She would . . . Edna's brain cried out to her to stop thinking like this.

She lay, tortured, on the bed for an hour; and then the sex bogey left her.

She remembered Brother Martin, and a sweet feeling filled her.

She rose and stuffed the money into the back pocket of her jeans. She got the basket from under the bed and gathered up the blanket. When she left the house, by the front way, her father and Elias and Gloria were making a row in the dining room. They would be drinking and playing cards until very late, and she would not be missed.

A hundred yards from the "Palace," Edna switched off the torch. The record player wasn't on, but there were voices. It was Edna's plan to get as close as possible to the house and wait for Brother Martin to seek her out there.

A slab of broken yellow light fell from the French window onto the patio. The Davidsons sat there over drinks with their guests, on cane chairs with cushions. Captain Davidson had his stiff back to Edna, but Mrs. Davidson faced her. The light coming from the house had washed the flashiness out of her hair and lips. There were no lines on her face. She held an unlighted cigarette in a holder. In her other hand was an insect "bomb."

Edna put down the basket and the blanket and squatted. She glanced over her shoulder into the heavy shadows. Brother Martin was out there, but soon he would crawl up behind her and tap her on the arm. Then they would move into the bush and she would hand over the things and they would say good-bye.

She returned her attention to the gathering on the patio. Mrs. Davidson was doing the talking now. Her cigarette remained unlighted and she waved the silver holder to make her points. Now and then she sprayed insect repellent about her.

Edna's ears were a bit slow to start with in picking up the words, but after a while they adjusted and she listened to what Mrs. Davidson was saying. The woman had a gritty voice. It was a confident voice, too, expecting to be heard without interruption or contradiction. And so she was. When-

ever the captain leaned forward with his lighter, Mrs. Davidson would flourish the holder or the "bomb," sending him
back.

". . . sitting for hours in the wood-and-iron lavatory at
the back, over the bottomless pit, or bucket, or whatever it
is they do have; sitting there thinking about life, no doubt,
and its meaning. Thank God, we have a French drain. I told
the Captain when he fancied becoming a big-game hunter
over long weekends, away from the heartless Exchange, and
we bought the farm and built this hideaway, I told him that if
the sanitary arrangements were not what I liked, wild horses
wouldn't drag me here. But they, they would feel lost without their black pit or bucket and those fat gray lizards on the
walls. And listen to this. A chicken is wanted for Sunday
dinner, so Ferris . . ."

Edna stiffened at the mention of her father's name.

". . . he lies in the passage in front of the open door with
a rifle and when a chicken passes by, he lets it have it. Bang!"

There was laughter. Captain Davidson boomed his encour-
agement, while the two others were more subdued, the woman
a trifle awkward, the man imitating his host, but not so ro-
bustly. Almost every sentence Mrs. Davidson spoke from now
on was rewarded with laughter, like a punctuation mark. It
was as if she anticipated it, and she would pause briefly until
the applause came, her eyes darting, and she could be released to go on.

"You may think it's amusing, but frankly I think it's sordid.
It's the girl I'm sorry for, really, despite how she's made a
pigsty of the lodge. You should see her—you will see her,
you're bound to if you buy the ranch. She's a wild animal,
but a beautiful wild animal; I must be honest and frank and
admit that. Has a quality that many of us would give a fortune
for. Two fortunes. A gazelle, an impala, maybe—that long
neck, those huge eyes. Fancy *me* saying all this. But you'll
see for yourselves. She'll be over this weekend no doubt.
I'm surprised she hasn't called yet; she's usually here five
minutes after we touch down. But then, of course, we rather
disturbed her little sanctuary, didn't we, so maybe she'll shy

clear for a while. She follows me around like a puppy-dog in her bare feet and regards me as if I were a visitor from another planet. I suppose I should be flattered, but it's a bore. Whatever you do, don't let her pester you if you take the place. She's easily got rid of; you needn't worry about that. All you have to say is, 'Go away, Edna.' And she'll go. They have no feelings to speak of.

"Just as well, considering all the skeletons in their cupboards. The first Mrs. Ferris I never met. She was long, long before my time, when I was a tiny little girl. *She* committed suicide, though it's hushed up. Father O'Leary whispered in my ear. The poor woman discovered right after the birth of her child that her husband had been carrying on with the local black beauties for years. Apparently he acquired this taste when he was quite young. A liking for a little black chatty-cat isn't that unusual in the Territory. It's not against the law. Anyway, to cut a long story short, the unfortunate first Mrs. Ferris went out of her mind and, the story goes, she rushed out into the veld and turned up rocks until she found a snake, which bit her. Like Cleopatra." The laughter here was strained, but Mrs. Davidson was not put off.

She clattered the bangles on her arms and went on. "They found her body days afterward, mainly due to the vultures in the sky. Now the second Mrs. Ferris, her I knew. My God. He married her about six years ago, soon after we'd bought the ranch from him, no doubt on the proceeds of the sale. He put the girl in a convent down south and off he went to Cape Town, on a spree. Back he came with this apparition. She was an excessively common woman, a tart, I've always maintained, he picked up in Adderley Street. Very ladylike, of course, genteel. She fell in love with the romantic name of Sherwood Ranch and pictured something green and lovely. I ask you. Ferris had led her to believe that he was well off. He hasn't two brass beans to rub together, not since the foot-and-mouth disease.

"At any rate, along came this bird of paradise into a land of crows—the second Mrs. Ferris, Evadne. Very dainty and with lots of grand ideas: a red sash and white gloves for the servant, antimacassars and doilies and so on. She once gave a tea party; it was a scream. I wish you'd been there. Still, I suppose the woman was making some kind of effort. I have never been able to fathom why she stayed so long—she left him little more than a year ago—because she must have known pretty soon about his carryings-on with black chatty-cat in the mealie field or behind the garage. That's common knowledge. Maybe she shared his dream about the money in the milk cans. Re the money: old Mr. Ferris, who died before I was even thought of, was rumored to be a rich man. And indeed he might well have been. But he dies, and no money at all is forthcoming, which causes a great deal of surprise up and down the Territory, so Father O'Leary informs me. Next thing, his son, our neighbor, announces that he has found a letter in his father's handwriting saying that he buried his fortune in cans in the veld. It's all very exciting, but hardly likely. Be that as it may, Ferris has fed himself on this hope ever since. Dig, dig, dig. You'll see for yourself—the farm is pitted with scars where he has been shoveling out the earth. I suppose it does give him something to do, keeps him occupied."

Mrs. Davidson paused to finish off her drink. She took up again, "Back to our beautiful doe-eyed Edna. I've known for a long time that she sneaks in here when we are away. Big Mac told me as much. I didn't mind—it must have made a change for her. But I mean, there are limits. She must have been in residence here for weeks, thinking she was safe because it's summer. We surprised her today; she hadn't a chance to clean up. I find one of my collection of porcelain birds smashed to smithereens—and lots and lots of other evidence. A filthy pink handkerchief with flowers. A bed slept in. My 'Blue Grass' in the dustbin. A mound of tins. God, she must eat like a horse. She leaves a trail of clues, silly girl."

Mrs. Davidson was finished. At last her cigarette was going. Smoke trickled out of her nose and mouth. The others broke into talk and Captain Davidson poured drinks.

Edna heard nothing more because there was thunder in her ears. She had had the skin stripped off her. She remained dead still for a long while, as though fearing that the slightest movement would cause her pain.

What Mrs. Davidson had said had damaged her more than she could tell. Seeing herself and her father through another's eyes had scarred Edna badly. She did not care what the woman had said about her looks.

She wanted to charge like a bull onto the patio and tear at Mrs. Davidson's throat. She wanted to drag herself into the bush and lie there until her wounds had healed.

However, all strength had gone out of her: she was weary; she did not move.

Edna had no idea how long she remained where she was. The Southern Cross was dropping out of the sky, an owl called, and nightjars churred. Somewhere an ostrich gave a roar like a lion.

Then Edna heard glasses and bottles knocking against each other on a tray and, slowly, with a great effort, she raised her eyes to see the people move off the patio into the house.

A hand with a glittering ring and long painted fingernails let down the blinds in the living room. Darkness leaped forward onto the patio.

Edna stayed where she was. Presently she heard a scuffing in the sand behind her, shoes treading lightly, but she did not turn round; she had no interest in who it might be.

A hand rested itself on her shoulder. "Miss Ferris?"

Edna took a deep breath and wondered if words would come. "Oh, so it's you," she heard herself saying in a listless voice. "I'd forgotten."

"I have waited for you all day! I knew you would come!" His voice was young. A man was down beside her in the dark, somebody who depended on her, needed her. She had but to lift her hand from her knee to stroke his hair.

"Did you hear?" asked Edna.

"Hear what?"

"You know—what she said. You were somewhere near all the time."

"I only heard bits and pieces," Brother Martin said.

Edna moved. She moved when she had imagined she never would again. Somebody had put a key in her back and was winding her up. Her voice, too, took on life. "My mother did not kill herself!"

"No, of course not. Naturally. Ssssh."

"How can she say that about my Dad? It was all lies, lies, lies!" Edna cried, wrenching a sentence out of her mind that was vaguely familiar, words she knew she had spoken in other circumstances. Her loudness startled her, and she hunched up, her spasm over. "But it wasn't all lies—some of it was true."

Captain Davidson was at the window, lifting up the blinds. "Is there anybody there, said the traveler?" he called. "Yoohoo. Come in, come in, whoever you are!" There was a pause. Edna found she was clutching Brother Martin's arm. "Tell them I came and no one answered, that I kept my word, he said." Captain Davidson let go the blinds.

"Come. Give me your hand. Let's go far away."

Edna had pins and needles in her feet. She pranced. "The blanket—the basket," she said. He went back to fetch them.

They ran, Brother Martin dragging her onward, across the airstrip to the spruit, the little river in which Edna had never seen water flowing. They jumped down the bank, and the cool sand crunched under Edna's feet.

After a bit, she began to cry. The tears were a luxury, a warm, salty release.

They were sitting on the sand—he had cleared a patch of branches and cow pats—and now he shifted toward her, awkwardly, and put an arm about her.

She wanted to slip her hands down to his hips and press him against her. For a second or two, her image of him as a brother was wrecked. But it reconstructed itself straight away.

"There will be a piccanin watching out there where we can't see him," said Edna, stirring. His eyelashes had brushed her cheek. She shoved gently.

With him there beside her, some of the hurt began to leave her. They were silent. But all too soon he got to his feet and said, "I must go."

"Not yet!" A bird woke up and flapped its wings. Edna cut her voice by half. "Not yet. Stay a little while longer. Look, I'll spread the blanket and you can have a rest. Wait for the dawn because there'll be snakes in your path in the dark."

They slept fitfully for some hours. Then the cold seeped up through the sand and a slight wind blew and this woke them fully.

"Good-bye," said Brother Martin. He kissed her on the cheek. There was the smell of milk on him.

He went away with the money and the blanket and the basket of food, heading in the direction of the main road.

"And good luck!" Edna called. She shone the torch for him, but he was soon out of its range.

When the bush had swallowed up the sound of twigs breaking under his feet, she wanted to shout out, "Wait! Come back!" She had an urge to run after him at the last minute. But she stayed where she was.

She was alone again. There was a weight of desolation on her, but after a while it eased. In a way, she felt she had grown up a lot.

The echoes of Mrs. Davidson's words began to fade in her mind, rejected by it. Edna felt stronger.

She did not want to return home, so she gathered some camelthorn branches and took the matches out of her back pocket and lighted a fire. When it was lively with flames, she went in search of a log from a dead motseara tree, which would burn slowly. This she tugged along the riverbed and put on the fire.

Termites scurried out of the inside of the spluttering log, and sparks flew and spat. Then it controlled itself and burned peacefully, forming a powdery white ash.

For what was left of the night, Edna stared into the wood coals. She saw no faces there—of people she knew or imagined —but only red shapes.

When the flat line that ruled off the east was turning gray, Edna kicked sand on the coals, suffocating them.

On her way home, she saw the spoonbill storks flying off to their daytime place. Near a waterless pan, she startled a buck. It galloped away.

Edna broke into a run, too. She did not want to be caught by the rising sun. She hated the day.

Five

✳✳✳ The Davidsons and their guests flew off to Johannesburg on the Sunday afternoon. Edna heard the plane zooming over the house and she blocked her ears. She was in her room, on her bed, where she had been all day, in a detached mood. Elias had stayed overnight, and now Mr. Ferris was giving him a tennis lesson. When the plane had gone, Edna could hear once more the plop of the tennis balls and Elias's shrieks.

Edna wondered idly how far Brother Martin had managed to get. She now thought of him only as Brother Martin of the Mission, running away. He had left the sphere of her life.

She was back at an earlier point: all she had to do was to get through as best she could the time between now and the examination results coming out. Then! Oh then . . . But her heart did not lift.

That evening Big Mac paid a rare visit, piccanins trailing him as he plodded over from the kraal with the fly whisk over his shoulder, his sign of rank. Through her window, Edna watched him approach and she decided, without alarm, that he must have come to tell her father that she had used the "Palace" for a fortnight. She was not concerned in any way. She would have an answer ready. When Elias saw his father, he climbed on his buzz-bike and left.

Big Mac had come to say, Mr. Ferris reported at the supper table, that the Davidsons were planning to sell the ranch, and their visitors had been potential buyers.

"Oh," said Edna, not interested.

She felt disassociated from everything.

This mood of hers lasted some weeks. It was as though recent events had drained her and she was storing up energy again. Her mind refused to face what she had overheard Mrs. Davidson say. It was impossible to believe that her mother might have done what that woman said she had.

Edna did not leave the house in the daytime. She wrote to eight new pen-friends. She completed her short story at last and posted it in longhand to the magazine. She made a new suit and a bow tie for the Teddy bear, and fixed up his eye.

Once or twice she went out late at night and built a fire in the veld and gazed into the coals, her mind empty. She scratched messages with her penknife on the fat branches of aloes. She drew hearts that had arrows through them, but she left out any initials.

One afternoon Gloria knocked on the door of Edna's room, and stepped back into the murky passage when Edna opened it. "What do you want?"

"Sweets, young madam, please, sweets for Gloria. I am so hungry for sweets." She had her hands cupped. Edna emptied some sweets—purple, green, pink, all scented—out of the glass jar and gave them to Gloria. When the girl had gone, Edna licked the stickiness from her fingers.

Christmas arrived, and Mr. Ferris and Edna drove to midnight Mass at the Mission, along an empty road. They always attended midnight Mass. Springhares went berserk in the path of the head lamps. Edna hated it when, blinded by the lights, they banged themselves to death against the truck.

The church was packed with bodies, but the heavy incense took care of the smell. Babies strapped to their mothers' backs wailed. There were flower aloes in tall gold vases on the altar. (Sister Clothilde sometimes spoke nostalgically of sprigs of lilac and hawthorn blossoms.) The candles wilted in the heat.

Mr. Ferris and Edna were ushered to the front, to share a row with the nuns. She looked about her for Brother Martin, but he was not there.

Those Natives who could not find a place on the benches sprawled on the floor. Many of them wore animal skins. An old man had porcupine quills stuck in his hair. A mother thrust her breast in the mouth of a noisy baby and silenced it. The body on the cross was bloodless and glistening. Edna could not bear to look at it.

There was a good deal of coughing going on in the stuffy church. But at last there was a hum, like a big bee, and the nun at the back, the very old one, was pumping the portable organ. The coughing dried up. The choir sang "Silent Night" in English, raucously and raggedly. Edna pictured snow and sleigh bells and pine trees and reindeer. Every year the choir sang "Silent Night."

The carol ended. A bell rang and Father O'Leary marched up to the altar in his gold-and-white vestments. Hands moved across faces and the Mass began. The ritual meant nothing to Edna. Once "Silent Night" had been got through, she lost interest in the proceedings. The Ferrises went to midnight Mass as a tradition.

They gathered afterward on the stoep of the convent to drink coffee and eat the nuns' sweet cakes. Sister Clothilde distributed Christmas presents, little articles she had made during the year. For Edna there was a pincushion in the shape of a lady in a crinoline, and for Mr. Ferris a pipe rack.

Father O'Leary gossiped and told jokes. Edna looked at him with dislike.

Nobody mentioned Brother Martin. It was as if he had never been.

Mr. Ferris and Edna got back to Sherwood Ranch after two. The truck swung into the driveway and the head lamps swept the blank face of the house. Elias appeared. He came dancing down the steps in a witch's hat. Somebody followed him.

"I have brought you a present, Archie! A crate of brandy. Let me introduce my new friend. Mr. Archie Ferris, Mr. Sixpence Bamangwa. Sixpence is in charge of stamps and postal orders."

"It is very late," said Mr. Ferris, hedging.

"How do you do," said the stranger. Sixpence had a party hat on, too: a sailor's hat with the words "Love Me, Sailor" sprayed on with gold dust.

"Oh Archie, don't spoil the fun," said Elias. A third person joined them, sliding out of the house, Gloria. She stood close to her brother.

Elias continued, "We have been to a party in Gowani and now we have come on to celebrate with you. All this way. Tomorrow is a public holiday and today. Poor Sixpence had to sit on the back with the brandy on his head. He fell off twice but no bottles broke because they are packed in straw."

"Ask them in," said Edna in a still voice. He would need them when she was gone; he would need friends then. For the first time she herself saw this. "Go on—ask them in," she repeated, as though her father had misheard her.

"Oh, the young madam," exclaimed Elias, pretending he had only just noticed her. "The compliments of the season and everything of the best for the new year."

"How do you do," said Sixpence.

The mantle of the lamp in Edna's room sucked the flame of the match she held and exploded into white. The eyes of the Teddy bear stared like a dead person's. Edna shook her pillow out of its slip and draped the slip over the end of her bed.

You never knew; he might steal in during the night and in the morning there would be a present.

In the morning, however, the pillow slip was empty. There was no present.

Snores rocked the house. But around midday, Mr. Ferris and Elias and Sixpence woke up and Gloria came over from her kia, treading heavily on the oily lines of heat in the yard. They took up their drinking again.

Edna remained in her room, reading a setwork book that she knew by heart. She was not interested in what was going on on the veranda, and she did not pitch her ears to try to catch what they were saying. She simply did not care; they could do what they liked.

In the middle of the afternoon, there was a drumming on

the door. There stood Gloria, looking bloated, begging for boiled sweets.

Toward evening, Mr. Ferris came with a hangdog expression, bringing brandy fumes into the room. "I appreciate your consideration," he said. He carried a glass of sweet wine and a plate with a slice of Christmas pudding on it. There was a moat of lumpy tinned cream round the pudding. He sat down heavily on the edge of the bed and some of the cream tipped off the plate onto the bedspread. Mr. Ferris scooped it up with his thumb and stuck his thumb in his mouth. "You must eat," he announced.

"I'm not hungry."

"You haven't eaten all day."

"I had some Post Toasties and rusks."

Mr. Ferris's eyes were concentrating on a point a few inches in front of him. His movements were slow, unsteadily steady. "You don't mind?" he said, waving a hand as if the air were syrup, in the direction of the veranda. "You really don't mind about them any longer?"

"No, I don't," said Edna.

He got up, smiling, relieved. "If you say so . . ." He halted at the door. "But it's good to know that you are here anyway, my girlie." Edna sensed him coming toward her and she looked up. "Give your old man a kiss, my girlie?" said Mr. Ferris. His lips had the texture of peeled grapes. She let him kiss her.

When the door had closed, Edna drank the sweet wine in one go.

The plate of Christmas pudding, the black fruit like lungs in it, stood untouched on the bedside table. The flies soon discovered it and settled on it. Some got their legs bogged and slowly drowned in the cream.

Edna read until the room was dense with shadows. She did not light the lamp.

The others grew rowdier; the setting sun had given them a new lease of life. The outline of the witch's hat appeared against the curtains and a nail scratched the fly screen. "Go away!" said Edna, and the hat ducked. Later, the buzz-bike was roaring round and round the house. Somebody must have let Oubaas off his chain because she heard him clattering on the roof.

Ordinarily, Edna would have gone for refuge across the veld to the "Palace." This would have been a good opportunity; nobody would have missed her. But she had sworn never to enter that house again. So there was nothing for her but to stay in her room.

The following morning, Boxing Day, she had a bath and went to the kitchen to find something to eat. The room was a mess. Some fowls had got in and were on the table, pecking at the unwashed plates. They flew off, squawking, at the sight of Edna. She opened a tin of peaches and ate them with a spoon, then drank the thick liquid.

She was weary of reading. As a diversion, she collected glasses on a tray and carried them to her room and arranged them on the floor. She filled the glasses with water, careful not to spill any. She drew open the curtains and lay on her bed.

In a bit, the light began to work on the water and make it frisk on the ceiling. She could watch this indefinitely. The jigging, quivering, leaping, interlacing patches of color fascinated her. Gazing at them, with eyes wide open or lids half-closed, made her mind a blank. For hours she watched the bright show on the ceiling.

Nobody else stirred until after midday. Then there were noises in the house. From the sound of them, the others were running down. The pace of the party had slackened.

Elias and his friend Sixpence left an hour before sunset. They took with them the chandelier. Sixpence, on the pillion, precarious, held it in front of him in a cardboard box. When she heard the calls of "Good-bye," Edna went to the window, hardly believing that the party could really be over. The ground was strewn with pieces of glass that had come loose from the chandelier, jewels in the dust. Mr. Ferris and Gloria stooped to pick them up. They dropped them, jangling, into the box that Sixpence held. When the buzz-bike started, rocketing forward, the Christmas hats came off the heads of Elias and his friend. The witch's one was a speckled black bird chasing after a dove.

Gloria had a fit of coughing, then silence stuck itself on the place. After a while, the bush noises came through, faintly to begin with, but then more confidently. Edna heard the Egyptian geese honking near the dam. She left her room and walked about the house to inspect the damage. There was litter everywhere: empty bottles, stained glasses, pieces from the chandelier, burned matches, cigarette stubs. Somebody had knocked over the rack of ferns and the plants were dead, flopped onto the granolithic floor of the veranda. There were dark dried spit stains, small irregular islands on the reddish concrete.

The door to her father's room was closed. Edna listened intently, bringing her ear against the keyhole, but she heard nothing. She shut one eye and, with the other, peered in. The curtains of the room were drawn and there was only blackness. But she knew they were in there, the two of them together, as surely as if a light shone on them.

She crossed the back yard to the kia. It was empty, as she had expected. But there were hundreds of people on the walls —in pictures: the Queen, film stars, pop singers, even the Pope giving a blessing. Gloria was not there.

On her way back to the house, a shape came at Edna out of the twilight and for a moment she imagined it was Brother Martin. The baboon circled her, showing his fangs. She picked up a stone and pelted Oubaas. He let out a yelp and cringed away. She'd have to get one of the boys at the kraal to catch him and put him back on his chain.

Mr. Ferris did not emerge from his room the next day. Edna set about spring-cleaning. She tackled the living room first, where the piano stood drunkenly. There was a bad smell in the shut-up room, and Edna found a rat that had eaten poison out of a saucer and burst. She swept the body onto a piece of paper and carried it to the bin in the kitchen. All morning she worked, throwing herself into the job, scrubbing, dusting, sweeping. But what she did made little impression. The living room (the parlor, Evadne Ferris had called it) looked pretty much the same as it had done before she had started. The decay had gone too far. You might as well write it off, she told herself. There was a white ring on the ceiling where the chandelier had hung, its empty hook a crooked finger now. You might as well put a match to the room, it looked so derelict. She closed the door. She never went into the parlor again.

Next, she cleaned the veranda. She polished the length and breadth of it and threw away the ferns. There was a gash in the fly screen where somebody had fallen against it. That would have to be fixed. But if you once began to think of all the things that needed fixing, there was no end to it, no end at all. It was terribly hot, working, and she was sodden. After the veranda, she went into the garden for half an hour and painted spots on the trees.

Eventually Mr. Ferris got up, after two days. He had on his old school tie and his sandals and gray socks. His face was fuzzy, and his hair wouldn't stay flat. He said, hitching up his leather belt, "Wasting precious time. Must get back to work."

"I've been trying to clean up the place, and I see the chandelier's gone."

"Oh, that. Oh, yes. What do we want a chandelier for when we haven't even got electricity? I gave it to Elias."

"To Elias? What could he do with a chandelier?"

Mr. Ferris lighted his pipe and dropped the match on the floor. Edna gave the curled black wire at his feet a long look. Mr. Ferris put his heel on the burned match and ground it away. "They say it's good for the carpet," he said. "As a matter of fact, I'm pleased you noticed, I'm pleased you asked. Shows you're taking an interest in the place, when all the time I thought you weren't."

"But to give it to Elias," said Edna.

"Don't sound so surprised. He said he'd always wanted a chandelier."

Mr. Ferris went back to his digging, and Edna began writing another short story. They resumed their tennis. One afternoon Edna heard thunder clearer than she had before that summer. At first she thought Gloria had dropped a tray in the kitchen, but then the sound was repeated, more muffled than plates breaking, stronger, rumbling, a baritone voice. She ran to the window. Away to the east was a range of black mountains, substantial, treeless, all rock, as high as the eye could see. Lightning flared in the crevices. She felt that she could almost smell rain in the dust around the house. But within half an hour the towering black precipices had dwindled to low gray hills and then these, too, were gone, evaporated, and there was nothing but the flat line of the horizon broken only by the spiky thorn trees. Nothing ever lasted long. Sometimes a hope of one kind or another was held out, but before you could grasp it, it was quickly withdrawn. There was no rain.

The Christmas beetles sawed into the brain.

Gloria killed a fowl on New Year's Eve. It was tough and sinewy from so much running about during its lifetime. The gravy was black and bitter and the potatoes were all crust and no flesh. The two crystal wine glasses were on the table, and there was some sweet wine left over from Christmas.

After dinner, Mr. Ferris and Edna sat on the veranda, waiting for midnight. A bottle of brandy was at Mr. Ferris's elbow. Even though the oil lamp was low, insects—some horny and noisy, others soft and silent—poured in through the gash in the wire mesh.

Mr. Ferris didn't appear to be interested in Edna's company. His eyes were out in the night, watching, perhaps, for the small bouncing moon of Elias's buzz-bike. Edna felt she might just as well not be there; hers wasn't the companionship he wanted. But when she said, "If you'll excuse me, I think I'll go to bed," he put his attention on her. He stopped her with a raised hand and said, "No, girlie, don't do that. Stay. We must see the New Year in together."

At midnight, they pushed back their grass chairs and stood up. They crossed their arms and held hands and sang "Auld Lang Syne."

In her room, Edna opened her notebook on a fresh page and printed, "NEW YEAR RESOLUTIONS." She smacked at a moth, which deposited a gray powder on her hand, like cigarette ash. Ten resolutions should have come easily off her ball-point pen, without her thinking, as they had always done in former years. But she could summon up nothing—no resolution, that is, that she felt would not be broken within a week. Never, at midnight on New Year's Eve, had a year lain ahead of her so devoid of good intentions. And this the year that was to be the most important, the most vital, in her life. She felt cheated.

The thought wriggled into her that, because she could find nothing to write down, maybe this would be the last year of her life. Death didn't breathe only on Mr. Ferris. Death stood briefly behind her, a thick waving cobweb, and she dared not turn round.

She stabbed the tip of the pen on her tongue to make the ink flow and wrote, quickly, not minding how the letters formed:

I, Marguerite de la Hunt, will keep to the best of my ability the following resolutions—

1. To make a great success of my new career as a radiographer.
2. To have clean thoughts at all times.
3. To beat my father, Mr. A. Ferris, at tennis.
4. To try to the best of my ability to fall in love.
5. Not to let anybody or anything upset me.
6. To be more charitable to everybody.
7. To complete my short story.
8. To improve my mind.
9. To improve my looks.
10. To stretch a piece of wire across the road and cause Elias to break his neck.

Edna put the cap on the pen, snapped shut the book, and went to bed. Her life flowed forward again. How different, she thought, next New Year's Eve would be. She would be attending a dance, and at midnight she and her partner would go onto the balcony and listen to the city greet the new

year: car hooters blasting, factory sirens wailing, people singing and shouting in the streets. No crickets or tree frogs.
Everything would be gay and full of life. She slept peacefully, lulled by this vision.

However, when the Matriculation results came out toward
the end of January, Edna learned that she had failed for the
third time.

Mr. Ferris brought her the news. He had been up the line,
to see about buying a rain-water tank from a farmer who was
leaving the Territory, and on the way back he had dropped
in at the Mission and Sister Clothilde had told him.

For so many years there had been a succession of set-
backs, but these she had been able to accept. This news,
however, was clearly beyond the limits of her endurance.
For a minute or more the passage reeled beneath Edna, and
she had to put her hands against the wall to prevent herself
from falling. She had read about bad news being a blow. This
was exactly how she felt, as if somebody had struck her
hard and repeatedly. There was nausea in her stomach and
her mouth was gummy.

She would have to start all over again. But at this moment,
another year on Sherwood Ranch was inconceivable. You
might just as well say ten years, fifty years, a hundred years.
"No, no," she moaned. "I do not believe you."

"Don't take it so hard, my girlie. It isn't the end of the
world. There are lots of people around who have never got
their Matric and have managed very well all the same. We
can't all be doctors or radiographers, you know."

Edna spoke slowly so as to conceal the cracks in her
voice. Her balance had come back to her and she was able
to stand. "It can't be true. It just can't."

"Life's like that, Edna."

"What you say means nothing to me," said Edna, moving
out of the house through the kitchen. "Absolutely nothing."
Mr. Ferris followed her. "Life can't be like that. I simply
won't believe it. I won't!" She stalked to the garage and got
into the truck. "Drive me to the Mission—I want to find out
for myself."

Sister Clothilde was praying in the church, and they had to wait a quarter of an hour for her to appear. Edna saw her gliding along the avenue of jacarandas, an iceberg, and she jumped out of the truck and ran to her.

"My dear," said the nun, "I'm so terribly, terribly sorry." Those words, once spoken, could never be taken back. Sister Clothilde was sentencing her to death for another year.

Edna felt her senses leaving her. A black wave crashed onto her. She pitched forward onto the indistinct white figure of the nun. "Help me, Mr. Ferris, do." Soft hands held her. She heard Sister Clothilde's voice at the end of a long tunnel. "Your daughter has fainted."

When Edna came to, she was on a chair on the veranda of the convent building with her head thrust between her legs.

Pictures flashed through her mind. She saw in succession Gloria's naked body in the moonlight, Oubaas scratching his tube, her father examining himself in the bathroom mirror, the pen-friend's drawing, the hearts she had carved on the aloes, the man in the advertisement, the glass eyes of the stuffed animals at the "Palace." Then the pictures became mixed up and there was great confusion, until at last Brother Martin stepped out of the eye of the black-maned lion and, lifting a hand, brought an end to the chaos.

Edna heard the nuns' alarmed, clucking voices all around her. Sister Clothilde's tough black shoes, sticking out from her habit, planted apart, were in front of her eyes, something to focus on.

"Here, drink this, my dear." Sister Clothilde eased her back in the chair and gave her a glass of water. Edna's hand shook and the water slopped, so the nun took the glass from her and held it to her lips. Edna disliked water from a plastic glass because of the taste; but she was too weak to protest, so she let some drops dribble into her mouth.

Gradually her surroundings came back to her. The old nun, the organist, the one with the face like a root, was close to her, a phantom in a dream. The women were making a sound like fowls again. Sister Clothilde shooed them indoors. Mr. Ferris was nowhere to be seen. Sister Clothilde was leaning over her, speaking to her gently in German. The foreign words were a lullaby and Edna's eyelids grew heavy. She would sleep, sleep, and then she would wake up and somebody would tell her it had all been a dreadful mistake, she had passed her examinations after all.

Sister Clothilde switched to English. "These things are sent to try us," Edna heard her saying. "They are all God's will."

"God's will," Edna murmured.

"Try to breathe deeply, my dear. You've had a shock." She felt the nun's hand on her; it was no longer soft but flaky. Edna grasped it and kissed it again and again, until Sister Clothilde withdrew her hand and put it in the folds of her sleeve.

"I'm all right now," said Edna, shaking herself. "Show me where it says I have failed."

Sister Clothilde fetched the handbook that contained the results. It had a green cover. She flipped over the pages. "There." The book was in Edna's lap, and the nun's finger, the nail a horn, was fixed to the top of the column of names of the successful candidates. "The Mission results begin here."

Edna's eyes fed on the printed names for some while. There was still a tiny hope. "But mine isn't here at all."

"No. No, it isn't. If a name is left out of the list, that means the candidate has failed." She was wheezing. "Beauty and Thelma failed; so did Dorothea. You weren't the only one. You'll just have to try again at the end of this year. You fall in this life, you simply pick yourself up and try again. Again and again, if necessary." Sister Clothilde knew she was using clichés, but they seemed to be the only appropriate words. She was upset and she wanted to help the girl, as she always had. She could only fall back on language that was worn and familiar.

"Why? Why are you all talking in this same way today?" Edna demanded. "Standing in your pulpits and preaching to me?"

Sister Clothilde, after giving her a quick sidelong glance, ignored what Edna had said, and continued, "I had so hoped you would be able to leave soon, but another year out of your life isn't so much after all. It may seem a bitter blow now—but it's nothing. You'll just try again. I'll help you."

"No," said Edna, through her teeth. She put her hands on the arms of the chair and lifted herself up. "No." The nun stepped back. "He has won!" The words spiraled out of her. "My father and the thorn trees and the jackals, they've got me where they want me."

Sister Clothilde turned pale. She took a small plastic bottle out of her sleeve and sprayed some of its contents into her mouth. "Don't excite yourself," said the nun. "I'll speak to your father. I'll tell him that some arrangement must be made so that you can leave. Perhaps you can go back to the Convent for a year?"

Edna calmed down a bit. "It's no good," she said. "It's too late now. I belong here; they'll never let me go."

Her surroundings closed in on her like a vise.

Six

❄❄❄ Toward the end of February, there was the gala opening of the farm stall.

Meanwhile, Edna had got rid of everything that reminded her of her former life—except the Teddy bear—in the belief that with these objects out of the way, she would forget what her life and its hopes had been like. The Teddy bear she couldn't part with. The rest she had destroyed: her books, her bundles of letters, the pictures on the walls of her room, her correspondence-college notes, the pincushion Sister Clothilde had given her. She made a pyre of them in the back yard and watched them go up in smoke. The fire— it was at night—shot sparks twice as high as the house. Oubaas barked. Mr. Ferris and Gloria stood on the kitchen steps, their faces burning in the glow; but they said nothing and did not intervene. The notebook containing Edna's New Year resolutions was torn up and pitched into the flames, too. A breeze arose in the night and scattered the ashes, and in the morning there was nothing to show except a black ring in the back yard where the earth had been scorched.

Edna took a pair of scissors and, sitting cross-legged on the floor, cut up her two dresses. She would not be needing those any longer. She worked on them systematically until they were nothing but shreds. Then Edna ripped down the curtains with their nursery figures and cut them up, too, into small squares. These she burned in the stove in the kitchen.

Everything Edna did, she did with deliberation. She was calm and slow; there was nothing frenzied in her actions.

One by one she was closing all the doors inside her, shutting herself up.

One day after lunch, she left the house and went into the veld beyond the earth dam, swinging her tennis racket at her side. Edna picked up pebbles, then stones, and hit them with the racket, sending them pinging away, until all the strings had broken. She hung the frame of the racket on the branch of a thorn tree, a weird decoration.

This was a Wednesday. Elias and Sixpence came now regularly on Wednesday afternoons for tennis, and then drinks and supper. They played what Mr. Ferris called American singles: two on one side against one on the other.

Edna collected a roll of barbed wire and a pair of pliers from the storeroom and she walked down the road toward the farm gate, about a mile. Only violet-eared waxbills were in the leafless mogonono bushes. The minute birds chittered when Edna passed.

She strung the wire taut across the track, binding it tightly to the trunks of trees on either side, at a level where it would slice into Elias's neck when he came along.

Having done that, she went back to the house and had a bath. She spent many hours in the bath nowadays, lying in the brown water until her skin crinkled, studying the wasps going in and out of their nest on the ceiling.

She heard the buzz-bike. It came right up to the front steps, and Elias called, "Archie, Archie, we're here! Where are you, Archibald Ferris?" So nothing could have happened. Her trap had not worked.

When it was dark, Edna went along the road with a torch to investigate. A puff adder moved off the track in front of her, where it had been warming itself in the sand. In the torchlight, its scales looked like autumn leaves.

Somebody had cut the wire. And that somebody was Elias, Edna told herself; he had always had sharp eyes.

The four of them were playing cards on the veranda. Edna could see the figures in the waving lamplight as she turned into the drive: her father thrown back in his chair, Elias in his porkpie hat, Sixpence waving his hands, Gloria hunched forward as she coughed.

Before, Edna would have avoided them by going round the back. But now she did not care one way or the other. She passed between the stone lions and went up the steps and through the fly-screen door.

Elias rose and tipped his hat. "Good evening, Miss Edna." He had never called her that before. For once, she thought she detected, there was nothing mocking in his tone either.

"Good evening," she replied.

"Where have you been, my girlie?"

"Out. Out for a stroll. Have you seen the stars? They're so lovely tonight." And she moved into the house. Her feet were dusty, so she took another bath.

Nobody mentioned the wire across the road.

Next thing, Mr. Ferris was up to something. The truck didn't set out in the mornings for Number Three Camp. It went east instead of west. Then for two days Mr. Ferris was shut up in the garage. Gloria went to and fro across the yard with cups of tea and occasionally a drink on a tray. Edna was not curious. And when Mr. Ferris eventually appeared in her room and said, "Come and see what I've made for you, a nice surprise," she followed him dutifully, without interest.

The garage doors were open and, as they approached, the first thing Edna noticed was the pots of paint. Then she saw the masonite sign. It was propped against the truck, painted in blue and white, the same colors as the beach umbrellas. The sign said:

ICE-COLD MILK

FRESH FARM VEGETABLES

TEAS AND MIXED GRILLS AT ALL HOURS

Mr. Ferris stood back proudly and, with a sweep of his arm, said, "Well, and what do you think of it?"

The last line didn't fit and the words "all hours" had had to be squeezed in, the letters tumbling over one another. In the four corners of the board, Mr. Ferris had painted flowers, each with four white petals and a blue center. The paint had run here and there.

Edna had forgotten all about her father's talk of opening a tea garden on the side of the main road for her to run; and she had imagined he had too. She had never expected the plan to go further than the buying of the umbrellas. (These had never been returned but were stacked in his room.)

With all his schemes Mr. Ferris was enthusiastic at first, but the enthusiasm soon died. He simply did not have the drive to carry anything through. Scattered throughout the farm were the relics of schemes he had abandoned: the brickworks, the motorcar graveyard, the quarry, the orange grove.

The bush, having been cleared, had speedily set about encroaching on them all, strangling the puny orange trees, burying the bodies of the old cars, pushing up through the kilns, reclaiming the quarry.

With the bricks he had hoped to make his fortune by supplying the building contractors when the Capital was going up, but the bricks turned out to be of a poor brittle quality and nobody would buy.

He had a week of fun with the quarry, dynamiting away, but then the Natives, usually docile, became threatening because, they complained through Big Mac, he was blasting on the site where their ancestors had buried their dead and was disturbing their spirits. (Edna had met some of these spirits in the veld; she had seen them clearly, warriors with spears.) A piece of flying stone gashed Mr. Ferris in the leg and the Natives nodded knowingly, as if this were a retribution; so he gave up the quarry.

The orange trees were expensive, and they came in tubs by road and rail from the Eastern Transvaal, six hundred miles away. Half of them were dead when they arrived at Gowani Siding. The rest Mr. Ferris planted on ground he had prepared for them. Here the question was irrigation. Nobody had paused to think of that. There was simply not enough water. Somehow a few of the trees survived for a year or two, losing their symmetrical shape, growing wild, but at last the veld conquered these sturdier ones as well.

The used cars were Mr. Ferris's most extraordinary scheme, and the whole Territory got to hear about it and laughed at him; but that didn't prevent them from selling their junked cars to him, and he paid out quite a bit for them. Mrs. Ferris was behind the venture. It was her artistic side coming out, she said. They were going to take off the doors of the broken-down cars and work panels of mosaics into them, bright and decorative as rickshaws, and sell these doors to the motor dealers in Johannesburg. Nothing came of it, of course. Before long, sand and mogonono bushes covered the cars. In the storeroom were the heavy wooden boxes packed tight with the sparkling colored chips that were to have gone into the mosaics. They had been ordered from Italy and had taken a year to arrive, far too late.

Edna remembered all this, not accusingly, but as a proof that whatever her father turned his hand to failed. He had the direct opposite of the Midas touch. And now he wanted her to run a roadside café. He had dredged up this plan again.

"It's for you I'm doing it, my girlie. I'm genuinely worried. You're not what you used to be. So I thought I'd find you something to interest you, to take your mind off yourself. The boys are busy building the place right now. They should have the roof on today."

Gloria was in the background, having a look at the board, craning her neck.

Edna said, "But you've put there, 'Ice-cold milk.' "

"And ice-cold milk it will be for the thirsty travelers! To-morrow I'm going to Peerbhay Brothers to buy a paraffin fridge."

"Paraffin fridges cost money."

"There'll be some cheap secondhand ones, sure to be." He could not be dampened, not in the initial stages.

But that, however, was not Edna's intention in putting up obstacles. Oddly enough, a certain interest was in her, where a few moments before there had been none. A feeling—the slightest movement of a leaf on a still day—a feeling of be-ginning again stirred in her.

Edna went on to the next items on the board. "The only fresh farm vegetables will be pumpkins and mealies, and maybe marrows. And what about the mixed grills at all hours? I would have to come home at night to sleep, and the place would be locked up. And if somebody stopped in the day-time and pointed and said, 'Look here, it says here mixed grills and I want a mixed grill,' what would I do then? I couldn't cook a mixed grill out there, not without a stove, and you can't advertise what you don't mean."

"Well, as a matter of fact . . ." Mr. Ferris halted and looked puzzled. His face brightened. "Well, if somebody did happen to stop and ask for a mixed grill—but I don't think they would, actually; I only put that in to make the place seem decent—you could always ask them to wait and come up here and get Gloria to cook a mixed grill."

"Three miles here and three miles back again, carrying a tray in the sun? Gloria couldn't make a mixed grill in any case. Not in a thousand years. A hundred thousand years."

"I suppose not." Mr. Ferris inspected the board. "I can paint the 'mixed grills' part out."

Edna, too, inspected the board, a finger on her chin. "No," she said finally. "Leave it in. Paint out 'at all hours' and then it will look more balanced."

Behind them, Gloria sniffed. "Pardon, but I can cook mixed grills," she said in Tswana. "I have been offered a job in the Capital, at the café. Elias told me. I want sweets."

Mr. Ferris swiveled round and, with a glare, sent her hurrying back to the kitchen.

Then he said to Edna, "So you will run it," not as a question but as an accepted fact.

At least it would take her away from the house itself. Edna nodded.

Mr. Ferris pulled in his stomach and patted it. "That's my girlie," he said. "I knew you'd soon be better, I knew it all along. I'll pop over and see how the boys are getting on. We'll have the gala opening at the end of the week. It's just as well I didn't send back the umbrellas."

The place was no more than a shack with a thatched roof

on the side of the main road, opposite the entrance to the farm.

Father O'Leary and Sister Clothilde and the old nun came to the opening, which was on a Saturday. The wind was gusty and captious, making dust devils spin like tops, a sign that there could be a so-oopwha. Edna saw the priest's small car trundle down the rise called Makagabe Hill, and she wished she hadn't cut up her dresses. She was in jeans and a shirt. "They're coming!" She smoothed her hands on her hips.

The twelve beach umbrellas had been stuck in the stony ground, giant blue mushrooms, and their canvas snapped and creaked. Grains of sand smacked against the signboard.

"Indeed," said Father O'Leary when he had handed the billowing nuns out of the car, "if this isn't progress." He stalked around the stall, examining it. "Very good. But the question is—will it pay, will it be patronized?"

On the counter was a pyramid of undersized knotty pumpkins and next to them a tray of marrows done up in cellophane packets. Father O'Leary pressed a finger into one of the marrows. "Too hard," he said. "Not enough moisture." He poked his nose into everything. The funnel at the back of the paraffin fridge was belching smoke. "What you must do," said the priest, "is fit a piece of gauze over the top so that insects don't fall down it. They clog the funnel and cause the smoke. I know all about paraffin fridges. If it refuses to work, stand it on its head and give it a kick."

There was a Primus stove in the stall and Edna made tea on it. A plate of sandwiches had been cut at Sherwood Ranch and Gloria had baked a cake. It sagged in the middle and the vanilla icing was lumpy.

Under two of the umbrellas were bridge tables and folding chairs. Mr. Ferris had bought these at Peerbhay's, along with the refrigerator. The Indians had donated a pack of beer for the occasion. Mr. Ferris and Father O'Leary drank straight from the pierced cans, because Edna had forgotten to bring glasses. The men sat under one of the umbrellas, Edna and the nuns under another.

"Ice-cold milk?" said Edna.

Sister Clothilde asked, "Have you started studying again?"

Edna had expected this, and she was prepared. "Since I last saw you," she began, and the remembrance of that time was bitter, "I have decided I don't want to be a radiographer. I don't want my Matric any more."

Edna heard Sister Clothilde's teacup clank in its saucer. "Can this possibly be the Edna Ferris I know who is talking, the Edna I have known since she was born?"

Father O'Leary called across, "That will do, sister."

For an instant, Edna was sure the nun was going to answer him back. She made a sucking noise and Edna saw her shoulders rise. But Sister Clothilde folded her arms and said, "I'll be pleased when winter's here. This has been one of our most trying summers." The weather was always an escape.

The piccanins found them out, coming the four miles from the kraal. They stayed on the opposite side of the road, by the pillars of the gateway, under the scrutiny of the stone lions on the top. (These lions were like the ones that slept at the bottom of the veranda steps of the house.) The piccanins played with stones and their toys made out of wire. They played mutely, politely, taking no notice of the Whites across the way.

When he had finished his second can of beer, Father O'Leary collected a glass jar from the cubbyhole of the car and sprinkled holy water on the stall. A few drops splashed on the marrows and ran off the cellophane like tears. "One thing I've noticed," said the priest, "and that is you have no stocks."

"Stocks?" said Mr. Ferris blankly.

"What you will trade in. Stocks of sweets and biscuits and mineral waters."

"Of course. Naturally. I didn't quite catch you. I have ordered sweets and biscuits and mineral waters from Peer-bhay Brothers." He looked at his watch. "They promised to deliver them by this afternoon."

Father O'Leary seemed doubtful, but he made no further comment. He said a prayer to keep snakes away from the stall.

"It was a lovely party," said the old, guttural nun. They shook hands all round, formally.

Sister Clothilde clasped Edna's hand and tried to send her a message through her eyes, but Edna refused to look into her face.

Father O'Leary dipped his hand into his right trouser pocket, and immediately the piccanins across the road were alerted. They stopped their games and stood still. The priest took out coins and separated the pennies from the silver. He flung the pennies into the air. The piccanins flew away from the gateway, screeching, and fell upon the money in the road. They groveled, scrambled, fought, bit, and kicked; all except the albino, who stood to one side, watching. Father O'Leary and Mr. Ferris rocked with laughter.

When the Volkswagen drew off, the piccanins chased after it for a hundred yards, shrill with excitement. They were swallowed up in dust. Soon Edna saw the blob of the car top Makagabe Hill and the hooter sounded three times in a farewell greeting. The piccanins trailed back. Their skins were powdery. They were counting their coins.

"Well," said Mr. Ferris, "that's that. I'll be getting along. There are things to be seen to."

What things? Edna wondered. She said, "I'll quickly wash the cups and I'll come with you."

Mr. Ferris looked appalled. "But you can't! You can't do that on the very day we open."

So Edna remained behind. Some of the piccanins hung onto the back of the truck for the ride home. The others continued with their games as if she wasn't there. However, Edna knew that they watched and recorded every move she made. She took a step forward and waved her arms. *"Hamba!"* They scattered behind the pillars, but a few minutes later they had filtered back.

There was a four-gallon plastic container for water, a tin basin, and a drying-up cloth. The fridge was pushing out more ugly smoke. Edna gave it a kick and, inside, the tin milk can shook. She began to wash up.

The western sky was a wall of dust, coming nearer every

second. A so-oopwha was charging in from the desert. Edna stood behind the counter and, helpless, watched it approach. Soon its sound reached her, the fierce wind ripping the thorn trees. The piccanins banked themselves against the curved wall of the gateway for protection.

"The umbrellas!" But before Edna had time to dash out and bring them in, the violent wind was upon her and the farm stall. The empty beer cans raced off, clattering across the stones. The wind uprooted the umbrellas and whisked them away, blue pennies whirling in the thick red dust.

Edna hung onto the pole of the umbrella nearest her. Sand blinded her and rasped her skin. It got into her nose and mouth. If there had been time, she would have tied a hanky over her face. She heard the bridge tables and the chairs shattering themselves. She was wrestling with the wind as if it were a person, a giant with a hot breath. She was not going to let go of this one last umbrella, she did not care if she was carried into the sky, right across the Limpopo into the Transvaal and dumped in a mealie field. Or if she was bashed against the stones. She was not going to let go. She was determined not to lose this umbrella. So she clung on with all her might.

The wind passed by; it subsided. It had not been a true so-oopwha after all, but it had done enough damage. The bridge tables and the folding chairs and eleven of the umbrellas were gone for good. You'd never see them again. The signboard had been dented and bruised by flying stones, and knocked askew. The dust had darkened the sky.

Once the wind had careened onward to the east, the piccanins crawled away from their shelter and ran home to the kraal. They were not going to risk being caught again. In a real so-oopwha you could be stranded for days, trapped where you were by the dense stinging sand, unable to find your direction.

This was not a good omen. Here was a sign that the farm stall was hardly likely to be a success. But Edna was resigned. Over the years, resignation had become part of her, forming unnoticed, like the hard skin under her feet.

So when Mr. Ferris said, "What nonsense, my girlie. We're too civilized to believe in signs. You're going to make a big success of the place, I can feel it in my bones," Edna merely shrugged. And she went back to the farm stall the following Monday.

Her father drove her there in the mornings. She took with her a can of milk and a round biscuit tin containing sandwiches that Gloria had cut the night before. The lid of the tin had on it a photograph of a fluffy white kitten with blue eyes.

By nine o'clock the sandwiches were dry and their edges had curled. The stocks of sweets and so on that Mr. Ferris had said had been ordered from Peerbhay Brothers never arrived. Edna did not bother to ask why.

The road that ran past the farm stall was straight and whitish, and the trees and scrub alongside it had a chalky look. The telephone line connecting the Capital with the south, a single strand looped from one fat wooden pole to another, made Edna feel in touch with the outside world. Sometimes she stood under the humming wire and imagined she could hear conversations.

From the stall, she could see the silver blocks of the water tanks at Gowani Siding. There, feathery karree trees grew because of the water. But in the vicinity of the stall was the usual dry bush. There was a small pan some distance off, a muddy depression surrounded by mimosas. Once or twice, toward evening, Edna took a stroll to the pan. There was little water in it and the ooze was printed with the hoofmarks of cattle. A dead tree stood in the middle and white tickbirds perched on its branches. Water turtles encrusted a rock like scabs.

Except for Natives on bicycles, very little traffic passed the farm stall; and what did was in a hurry to get somewhere else, so nobody stopped. Edna did not mind particularly. She would rather it was this way.

As soon as she arrived at the stall, she put up the umbrella and arranged under it a grass table and two chairs that had been brought from the house. Then she pumped paraffin into the fridge and fiddled with the wick to try to stop the smoking. The fridge was moody. Always there was smoke of some kind: sometimes a thin thread, which didn't worry her; at others wads of black smoke thrust themselves out of the funnel, and she had to go outside to avoid choking. The piece of gauze over the top did not seem to help much.

In a way, Edna was glad to have the farm stall. It took the place of the "Palace." It was her hide-out. Here she could sit for hours with her disordered thoughts, without fear of being disturbed. As a child she had spent a good deal of time under her bed or in the cupboard with the door closed, imagining she was secure. The "Palace" had served a similar purpose; and now the stall was a substitute for it. It was her world away from Sherwood Ranch. She was pleased to be able to go there each day, too, because this meant she would not be bumping into Gloria wherever she moved in the house. Turn a corner in the passage, enter a room, Gloria always seemed to be there these days, flaunting her growing belly.

For lunch, Edna ate some of the sandwiches and drank a glass of milk. What was left of the sandwiches she threw to the piccanins. Always there were some of them playing at the gateway, all day long. If they could, they traveled clinging to the back of the truck.

Most of the time, Edna sat in the darkest corner of the stall. There was enough light to play patience by. Sometimes she took cubes of ice out of the refrigerator and rubbed them on her legs and her face until they melted.

Her ears were as sharp as ever. Whenever she picked up the sound of an approaching vehicle, far away, she would will it not to stop, would pray that it would pass. It always did, tearing north or south, chucking up stones.

The railway line was less than a mile away, to the east. The sound of a train had a different effect on Edna. Whenever she heard one in the distance, she would leave the stall and stand on a boulder to try to catch a glimpse of it. The piccanins took to the top of the wall for their view. In the daytime, there were only goods trains. The passenger train to and from Rhodesia went by at night, a string of lights, an exotic necklace, to spare the travelers the heat and dullness of this land when the sun was up. Edna loved the sound of a train's whistle and the whining and clanking of its coaches on the rails. Even though she had now, after her breakdown, resigned herself to not leaving Sherwood Ranch—she had in fact come to believe that she had been predestined for the Territory— the sound of a train could still make her picture that she was on it, going away.

She stood then on the boulder and breathed in deeply, try- ing to catch a whiff of sulphur from the engine's smoke. This was healthy, good for the lungs. Once she saw a line of cars straddling the backs of the trucks of a train, firm new colors, a flash of chrome, an orderly line of traffic moving across the tops of the karree trees, thirty cars headed for showrooms.

As soon as a train had gone, Edna hurried back into the stall.

She began, after a while, to take up familiar threads. She had rummaged out pieces of material from Mrs. Ferris's work- basket, and she made more clothes and bow ties for the Teddy bear, hurting her eyes in the weak light. Six of the eight new pen-friends had replied, in due course, and she wrote back to them, ten-page letters, all identical.

Mr. Ferris came to collect Edna every evening. The Ford chugged through the mogonono bushes.

"Any customers?" Mr. Ferris would ask while Edna was taking down the umbrella.

"None. Two cars went by." Or, "An ox wagon and a truck." The hood of canvas collapsed over her. She got her head out. "And you—any luck?"

"None."

One evening, Mr. Ferris said, "I'm finished with Number Three Camp. There's obviously nothing there. Tomorrow I'm starting on the riverbed. Earth-moving equipment would have been a help for that."

"The riverbed?" asked Edna in a tone that implied that he could not have meant what he had said. He was looking tired these days, and the purses of skin on his face were looser.

She would have said he was losing weight, except that his paunch showed as much as before. "The riverbed?" she repeated.

"Where else?" Mr. Ferris shrugged. "For twenty-five years I've been searching, and where else could the milk cans be?"

The day Mr. Ferris and his gang from the kraal began digging in the riverbed, Edna had her first customers. Elias and Sixpence jogged up to the farm stall on the buzz-bike. By this stage, the machine was a wreck. Bits of wire held it together.

Elias and Sixpence were in tennis clothes. Elias wore a red peaked cap. It was a Wednesday and they were on their way to Sherwood Ranch.

"Hello, Miss Edna," said Elias. "I am so sorry to hear you did not pass your Matric, but next time better luck."

"There isn't going to be a next time," said Edna with finality.

"How do you do. Hot enough for you?" Sixpence was standing back, rather bashfully, but when Edna nodded at him in acknowledgment he came forward eagerly, like a puppy-dog. Elias stopped his advance by motioning him to the table under the umbrella. Elias also took a seat. He said, "Me and Sixpence are hungry, and we would like a mixed grill, if it is at all possible."

Sixpence was picking his nose. "Stop that!" Edna rapped at him, and he looked startled.

"Yes, certainly, Miss Edna."

She placed her hands on her hips and said, "The mixed grills are off."

"In that case," said Elias, "can I see the menu?"

"There was no menu, there is no menu, and there never will be a menu."

"God Almighty, Miss Edna, it is so silly to go on like this. When are you and I going to be friends? Once upon a time we were, when we were tiny. If we were friends now, we could all play bridge and have hanky tournaments."

Edna kept her mouth shut and stared straight ahead of her. She wished she had a sjambok hanging behind the door.

No wonder so many Whites were clearing out of the Territory.

Elias sighed and said, "Well, then, Miss Edna, if there's no mixed grills, what can you offer us?"

Edna had not yet had her lunch, and the sandwiches were in the biscuit tin. "Ice-cold milk and cheese sandwiches," she said. "Take it or leave it."

"For two then, please, if you don't mind."

From inside the stall, Edna watched them. They ate daintily, like cats, and before they drank they clinked their glasses together. When they were finished and had wiped off their white moustaches, she went out and said, "That will be one pound, thank you."

Neither Elias nor Sixpence gave any sign of surprise. Elias felt in his back pocket and brought out a pound note, which he held in front of her in the tips of his fingers. Edna snatched it away. The men rose and crossed to the buzz-bike, which was leaning against a boulder. "So long," said Elias.

Edna cleared the table. Under one of the plates lay a shilling. She glared at it. Then she picked it up and pitched it across the road to the piccanins. They went wild. They had never fought for a silver coin before.

Edna folded the pound note into a neat wad and stuck it into her breast pocket. That night she smoothed it out, slipped it into an envelope, and locked the envelope in the top drawer of her desk.

Edna missed her tennis, but she would not admit this to her father. She found an old warped racket in the storeroom—Evadne Ferris's it had been, and five of the strings were gone. She sneaked it and a box of balls to the farm stall and now and then she practiced her shots against the wall away from the road. The piccanins scampered after the balls that flew about, retrieved them, and brought them back to her.

One afternoon, Edna was in her corner in the stall, dabbing at her face with a piece of ice, when she heard a car bearing down from the north. At first she did not take much notice —the vehicle would hare past, like all the others—but then her ears told her that the car was slowing down. Gears grated, the engine ticked over, the car had stopped. Edna ran outside.

Father O'Leary was getting out of his Volkswagen. His face was freshly shaved, marked with smears of talcum powder, and he had on his black suit, his black shiny square-toed shoes, and his dog collar. "And how's the big enterprise, the tea shop, getting on?" he sang as he came up to Edna, stepping high in the dust because of his polished shoes. "You are well, I hope?"

On the back seat of the car, Edna caught sight of a suitcase and a traveling rug. They shook hands, his hand crushing hers.

"But where are all the umbrellas?"

"They blew away," said Edna, gesturing to the east. "Way over there. I saved one."

"Oh, well. These things happen. And how is the refrigerator?" He explained to her again what to do when it smoked.

The piccanins looked on hopefully.

The suitcase had made Edna suspicious. She asked Father O'Leary directly, "Where are you going?"

He was about to answer her, and then he checked himself and said vaguely, "On a little trip, over the hills and far away. I must get through the Customs by eight. They close the gates at eight, don't they?"

Edna watched the small red car scramble southward, twining a rope of dust behind it. She sensed that Father O'Leary was on his way to Durban to fetch Brother Martin. Something must have gone wrong.

You couldn't escape, there was no point in trying, Edna told herself. Even if you got beyond the borders of the Territory, the place sent out its tentacles and drew you back in the end, jealously, after a month or two months or a year or longer. It wouldn't surprise her if Evadne Ferris forgot about her divorce and returned one day. If the Territory wanted you, it got you.

To think that Brother Martin had been defeated made Edna sad.

That night, she decided she would take up knitting as a

hobby. Evadne Ferris had shown her the rudiments, how to cast on and do plain stitches. There were balls of yellow wool in the storeroom. Fish moths scurried out of them.

"What on earth are you doing?" said Mr. Ferris.

"I am making you a scarf for winter." When the wool snapped, she tied the pieces together, biting off the loose ends, with the result that knobs appeared in the scarf. The color of the wool changed as she knitted, became dirty, no matter how often she washed her hands. Her fingers smudged the wool as it grew like chain mail on the rod of the needle.

She took her knitting to the farm stall and concentrated on it all day. When the wool at length ran out, the scarf was six feet long and one end, the end she finished last, was ten inches wider than the other.

By this time, Father O'Leary had been gone a week. Edna rolled up the scarf, skewered it with a needle, and pulled her chair to the counter.

He should be coming back soon. She kept her eyes on the road from the south.

When, two days later, she saw the Volkswagen nearing, she stepped hastily out into the road and waved her arms. The car slowed, but she could tell that Father O'Leary had no intention of stopping.

The car veered to the left, and she skipped in front of it, a hand up in a stop sign. The front bumper was a foot away from her when the Volkswagen came to a standstill. Father O'Leary thrust his head out of the window. "What is it now, Edna?" he said. "I'm in a hurry."

She had not thought of any excuse for stopping him; she would have to make up one quickly. But her purpose of leaping out into the road had been served. She saw what she had been certain of.

The confirmation was there. In the passenger's seat was Brother Martin.

"I wonder if you could give a message to Sister Clothilde, please?" Out of the corner of her eye, she took in Brother Martin. He appeared to have shrunk, but that could have been due to the way he was sitting, slouched down. His body seemed to have drawn in from his clothes, which were loose on him, as if they were on a hanger. His eyes, too, had receded. They were fixed on his hands, which were locked together on his lap. His cheeks, however, were the same—a bright, almost artificial pink; and his dark hair was glossy. Sunlight was on it and made it look like coils of stone, chiseled hair.

"Oh, hello there, Brother Martin," said Edna. He glanced at her swiftly, with empty eyes. She had hoped to find a message in them, but they were blank, without even a sign of recognition.

"Really, Edna," said Father O'Leary impatiently. "What message?"

Just in time, something arrived in her head. "I was wondering," said Edna, "if you'd tell Sister Clothilde from me that I've decided to have another go at my Matric after all."

The priest nodded curtly and put the car into gear. Edna stole a last look at Brother Martin. His head was low, a schoolboy in disgrace, and she noticed on the crown a small patch of skin. One day he'd most likely be bald.

The car shot forward, and with this abrupt movement Brother Martin's body wobbled, as though he had no bones.

Edna's eyes followed the car until it had disappeared over the top of Makagabe Hill.

She was filled with a gnawing vacant feeling. What Brother Martin had tried to do had been of no use, had been doomed from the start. In a little while, he would be back in his room in the priest's whitewashed house, a prisoner once more.

A cold worm crawled down Edna's back. The man, her friend, had not seemed to know who she was.

A mood of depression began to settle on Edna. To try to fight it, she went into the farm stall and occupied herself with unraveling the long scarf. She would make another start on it, having learned by her mistakes, being sure this time that it remained the same width and was not perforated with dropped stitches. She would wear gloves, too, while she knitted, for cleanliness.

Not long after the Volkswagen had gone, Edna heard another vehicle approaching. It was traveling fast, shooting up stones. Then, all of a sudden, there was a bang and the car began to reduce speed and there was a clanking sound. The car came to a halt a few yards from the farm stall, and Edna went to the door and looked out.

The car was an American make, plump, two-toned, slightly lopsided now at the back. A tire had burst. Two men were in the car, their faces smears of exasperation behind the windshield, a White man and a Black one, both in dustcoats. The back of the car was packed with dark brown cardboard boxes. It had a Johannesburg registration.

The men got out. Edna watched silently, half in and half out of the stall, as the two of them set about changing the wheel. By degrees the inquisitive piccanins closed in, moving one step at a time; but only going so far and no farther. The men sweated, and the onlookers were still.

When the good tire was on, the White man looked up at Edna and the farm stall for the first time, as though he had only just registered them. Then he came directly across to Edna, walking lightly, springily. He was thin and tall and he held himself erect, not in the way Captain Davidson did, stiffly, but naturally.

"Good morning," he said, and his voice was soft. Edna had somehow expected it to be harsh. All voices in the Territory were inclined that way. "What a God-forsaken place for a blowout." He waggled his hands in front of him. His fingers were long. "I wonder if you could let me have a drop of water to wash these in?" He glanced at his hands as if they displeased him to some extent.

The man's hair was brownish, a nondescript color, and it was cut short, without a parting. It fitted him like a cap. His eyes were green and the lashes were thick. His eyebrows were an unbroken dark line, joining on the bridge of his nose. One eye was fractionally lower than the other, so his face gave the impression of being slightly tilted to one side. His nose was long and straight, and his lips were narrow, but at the ends they turned up and not down. He had an open, pleasant face.

Curious things happened to Edna. There was cleanliness in the air. She smelled the sea and she heard waves flopping on the sand; and then the sound of the waves faded and the "Toreador Song" took its place, softly to begin with, but gradually mounting until it filled her head. She thought of a bird in a cage being set free. She became aware of a weightlessness in her, as though she herself could drift into the sky at any moment. Her skin tingled. There was no time to work out what these sensations meant, but a voice said clearly in her that some kind of crisis in her destiny had been reached. She was absolutely sure of this. She was certain that in all her life no moments had had as much importance as these during which she kept her eyes focused on the man.

It was only when he coughed and repeated his request that Edna realized she had been staring at him, as if he were a specimen, a picture in a magazine, something that was unconscious of her prying eyes on it. When he spoke, asking again for water to wash in, she blushed. She wondered if he could have read what had been going on in her.

But he smiled at her, neutrally, and she felt at ease at once. His two front teeth overlapped slightly.

"Of course," said Edna. "What am I thinking of?" She filled the basin from the plastic water container and placed the basin and a drying-up cloth on the counter. "Oh, dear," said Edna, flustered. "I forgot the soap." She handed him a bar of Lifebuoy and he took it in his long fingers. He washed carefully, creaming his hands, and he dried them thoroughly, even the webs between his fingers. He swilled the basin and splashed the water onto the dry earth. Then the man asked if Fred could wash, and Edna said, "But of course." She poured in more water. He carried the basin, the towel, and the soap to the car, where the Native waited. When the man came back, he said, "Thank you for your kindness," in a polite, old-fashioned way.

Their short encounter showed signs of entering its final stage, and Edna did not want it to end at all. It was impossible that it should. She said, rather urgently, "Would you care for a glass of milk?"

The man hesitated. "I don't know," he replied, doubtfully. "I have to be in the Capital by nightfall."

Edna laughed with relief. "You must be new in these parts then," she said. "Even in my dad's old truck, the Capital's only three hours away."

"This is my first trip hereabouts, as a matter of fact," the man said. He smiled once more. "Very well, I'd love a glass of milk."

"Oh good!"

Edna signaled to him to take a seat at the grass table under the umbrella, in the splotch of warm shade.

She had a setback when she opened the fridge. Unnoticed by her, the paraffin had run low and the flame had gone out. The fridge was defrosting. Water dripped sluggishly into a pool at the bottom, and what ice was left on the side of the deep-freeze was smooth and glassy from the thaw, no longer crisp and frosty. The milk was thick in its can, sour. She had a moment or two of anxiety; then she spied the bottle of Oros on the counter, with a few sticky inches of orange drink left in it. This she shared out among three glasses—one for Fred—which she topped up with water. She arranged some sandwiches on a plate and she carried everything out on a tray. But before she left the stall, she combed her hair with her fingers, setting it as best she could in wings on either side of a crooked center parting; and she bit her lips and pinched her cheeks to make their color healthy. She wished she had a mirror she could look into. On the other hand, she was glad she hadn't because of the apparition she might see.

"I'm so sorry," said Edna, "the milk has gone sort of curdly. The heat, you know, it spoils everything. But I hope a cool drink will do, and there's one for Fred as well." Fred came over to collect his drink and sandwiches and returned to the car.

"The trouble is," Edna continued, sitting down and taking care how she placed her legs, "that after nine o'clock the sandwiches turn up at the edges, which is a dreadful pity. It's the terrible sun. If I had the choice, I'd like to live in Switzerland or somewhere where there's snow." In Edna's ears, her voice sounded unfamiliar and brittle; and then she realized she was trying to imitate Mrs. Davdison, not only in the way she spoke but also in how she had her legs crossed with one hand draped over the knee and the other in readiness for gesticulations.

As soon as this occurred to Edna, she dropped her pose. She uncrossed her legs and put her hands between her knees. She said, "There's Marmite or cheese, whichever you like. I'm sorry the lettuce has gone brown. I'll be so thankful when the summer is over."

The man passed the plate to Edna, and for the first time she noticed his ring. She wondered why she had not spotted it before. The ring was a chunky square of gold studded with small diamonds in the form of a P. It must have cost a good deal of money; but it didn't go with him somehow, didn't fit in. He was too austere for this flashiness. "Ta," said Edna, picking up a sandwich. "Do you happen to be married?"

He saw where her eyes were and he turned the ring round on his finger so that only the narrower gold band of the back showed. "I'm not married. It was a gift."

"From a girl friend?" asked Edna. She took a tiny, delicate bite off the tip of her sandwich.

Furrows appeared on the man's forehead, but they soon went; and his crooked teeth showed. She liked his smile. It didn't make her uneasy, as Brother Martin's could, though there was something similar between the two smiles; they both had a likeness to a nervous tic.

"That's right," the man replied. "From a girl friend," he added, distantly, dreamily, in a manner that made Edna think that this particular girl must be overseas, far away, or even dead.

"I'm so sorry," she said.

It was now his turn to examine her closely. Thus far, Edna felt, she might have been no more than a shape; but now she sensed his eyes on her, and her skin stiffened and she tilted her chin. It wasn't fair; if she had had any idea that the day was to hold this inspection for her, she would have done something about her appearance that morning. But how was she to guess that a stranger was to arrive out of the blue and look her up and down?

There was a long silence as the man's eyes roved over her, and at last Edna felt compelled to move her head because what if the hour changed, a clock struck somewhere, and she was frozen in this position? So she shifted, and her eyes met his. He was watching her intently, almost boldly. His green eyes were like the sea.

She said, "Are you by any chance Jewish?"

The color of the skin just beneath the man's hairline altered, whitening. This she noticed.

He turned his head to one side, away from her. His profile was sharp. There were creases in the skin of his neck, so he couldn't be very young. "Why do you ask?"

"My dad says that all commercial travelers are Jewish."

"He does, does he?" the man replied. From his tone, Edna knew she had offended him, and she regretted that she hadn't stopped to think. Mrs. Davidson had called her insensitive; perhaps the woman was right after all. But Edna's question had been wholly unintentional. How could she convey this to the man without getting further into a mess? She went hot and itchy under her arms. She wanted to scratch herself. The man's "He does, does he?" hung in the air, displaced, waiting to be answered.

He flicked a cigarette out of a packet of twenty and held to it a lighter like a fat pencil. This, too, was of gold. After he had inhaled, he said, "No—I'm not Jewish. But I am a commercial traveler."

"Oh," said Edna. "Oh. That's most interesting."

"Interesting?" There was incredulity in his voice.

"Well, you see, I've never actually met a proper commercial traveler before."

There was a moment of considerable strain, and Edna was convinced that the man would be going now, at once; she had lost him as she eventually lost everything—her long line of pets, her friends at the Convent, Brother Martin.

The man moved a finger round the inside of his collar, as if his tie were choking him. She watched him apprehensively, her breath pinned in, and when at length a grin took over his face, she sighed and closed her eyes briefly. Whatever the crisis had been, it was over.

"Do you know," he said, "I like you."

There was a buzzing in her head. She couldn't have heard him correctly. "What?"

"I like you." He spoke casually. "You're a funny girl."

At this instant, Edna's life opened up again, like a flower. The wheel of her experience began to turn once more. She felt refreshingly cool. She could have got up and danced down the road, on the lake of heat waves.

The man stripped off his dustcoat and hung it over the back of the chair. He loosened his tie and undid the top button of his white shirt. The tie was a narrow black one with a short fringe at the bottom, austere, except for a small P done in silver. His cuff links were gold coins with an emperor's wreathed bald head. He sat with his legs wide apart. There was something there—not just folds of cloth, as with Brother Martin. "Tell me," he said, placing his elbows on the table, "tell me something about yourself. What are you doing stuck out here? Where do you come from?"

"There's really nothing to tell." However, she filled in some of her life for him, hesitantly, unsure of herself, dismissing whatever she said with a shrug and an uneasy, rather high laugh. But he seemed genuinely curious. Boredom did not make his eyes stray. He watched her closely. What's more, he prodded her with questions. Nobody had ever shown this kind of interest in her before. After a while, her uncertainty vanished. Talking to him was exhilarating; she was lifted out of herself.

Eventually she ran down; there was nothing more she wanted to add at this stage. You couldn't tell your secrets to a perfect stranger. "And what about you?" she asked.

This question sent him halfway into his shell. "Nothing," he replied. "I am a chemist by profession, but I've become a commercial traveler—in medical goods."

"You have?" said Edna. "Isn't that a coincidence, because

I was going to be a radiographer. Why did you change from being a chemist?"

"More money. The times, you know. I'll be doing this part of the world every once in a while."

"How often?" The two words rushed out of her.

"Twice a year, maybe."

Edna bit her tongue. Twice a year. She could not come to grips with time, she loathed the necessity of time, which others seemed to accept, speaking of a day, a week, six months as if somehow they were all equal quantities; you simply sprang from one to the other with nothing tripping you up in between. She would like to take up all the clocks and watches she could get her hands on and smash them to pieces. She glowered at the watch on the man's wrist. It had a gold strap and the links were like the scales of a fish. She could see the long slender second hand jerking past the black strokes on its face.

"Twice a year. That's not very often," said Edna. She brightened. After all, she had to grasp what she could get. "But you will stop here whenever you pass by, won't you? You won't wait for another blowout?"

"Surely." He was rising, shaking out his dustcoat. He had been there more than an hour, and Fred was making impatient signs from the car. "I'll come back in about a fortnight." The edges of his mouth rose. "For ice-cold milk?"

"I feel so ashamed," said Edna. Then she laughed. "Next time, I promise, the fridge will be working."

The man's hand had gone into his pocket for something. The piccanins stirred. When Edna realized he was going to bring out coins, she said, "Please. Please! Don't pay me. It was such a pleasure. I loved having you here." And, once the words were out, she reddened. Edna tried to extricate herself. "It's so seldom that I meet people to talk to. I mean, the ordinary people who pass by, if they stopped, I'd make them pay. . . ."

"Why, thank you, then." He was close to her and, without warning, he raised a hand and gently placed the back of it against her cheek. She moved her face and pressed her lips on his knuckles. Her teeth met the ring.

Take me with you, her heart cried out, take me with you in your two-tone car wherever you go! I can squeeze in among the sample cases at the back; I won't be a nuisance. Won't you do that for me?

The man slipped his cool hand away. "My name is Peter," he said. "Peter Westgate. And yours?"

"Mine?"

"Your name?"

"Well," said Edna, "as a matter of fact, my name is Marguerite—Marguerite de la Hunt."

Seven

❋❋❋ The man had said he would be coming that way again in about two weeks, perhaps a bit longer, returning to Johannesburg after his tour of the Territory. Edna kept her eyes on Makagabe Hill for the car. She moved the umbrella to that side of the farm stall and sat under it all day, watching for a sign of the vehicle. She tried to keep her feelings subdued, not to raise her hopes. She had suffered disappointments far too often by now not to make some kind of insurance against loss. There was a possibility, she announced to herself, that he might not come back that way at all. There was a border post to the north of the Capital, on the Limpopo, and there was nothing to prevent him from crossing into the Transvaal that way. And yet, the other side of her argued, the side where her dreams were stored, he had said he would come back; and she trusted him.

Beyond that—calling in at the farm stall for five minutes, washing down the dust with a glass of milk, exchanging a few words—there was nothing she could expect or demand of him. She had no claims on him whatsoever. He was a stranger, a commercial traveler who had happened to have a blowout on her doorstep. If it had not been for that accident, the car would have gone streaking on to the Capital and she would never have met him at all. It was pure chance that she had, a stroke of luck. But she shouldn't talk about luck, either; that was being superstitious—and she was done with superstition, along with false hopes. She would give up crossing her fingers, throwing spilled salt over her left shoulder, bowing three times to the silver hair of a new moon. She was done with superstition for good. From now on she would sleep with the moon on her face if she wanted to, would cut her nails on Sundays, would eat the marrow of pork. This was the way the practical side of her ran. And yet . . .

And yet, though nothing had been said to encourage her beyond the fact that he liked her and thought she was a "funny" girl, Edna began to build a fantasy. The man was her knight come from the east to rescue her, that was how she saw it. She pictured herself as the heroine in a magazine story. In that framework, there were certain rules that applied, the same way that in a fairy tale the good people lived happily ever afterward. She paused for a moment to consider what harm fairy tales could cause, how unreal they were; but she went on quickly from there, discarding this consideration, and plunged herself into a dream of her own. Her mind colored it romantically. There would be ups and downs, misunderstandings—yes, like in the stories—but in the end, maybe even as late as the final paragraph, Peter Westgate would propose to Marguerite de la Hunt.

Sister Clothilde was her ally; the nun wanted her to get away from the Territory. But Edna knew that if she had gone to the Mission and told Sister Clothilde how this portion of her mind was weaving this fabric, the nun would have warned her immediately of the dangers. Life wasn't like that. That was the nun's doctrine. Being romantic exposed you automatically to hurt. You had to build up a protection. Life didn't follow a pretty formula.

But why, asked Edna's inner voice, why couldn't life be like that? Just for once.

All the same, she would have to be careful. There was some wisdom in what Sister Clothilde had tried to instill in her. She had no reason to expect anything from Peter Westgate; he meant nothing to her. But she trusted him. Her ability to trust, once so badly damaged, had been restored to her.

Edna waited. Waiting had become a condition of her life: annulling time was the difficulty.

She sat and watched the north all day with eyes that never

shifted, not even when a goods train clanked by on her right.

Toward the end of the fortnight, doubt began to form in her like a growth, causing her an actual pain in her side. She wondered if she had already gone too far, raising her hopes beyond the point where her disappointment would not be so bitter if he did not come back. In her worry, she bit her arms, making blue marks with red rings. Warm tears drummed against the backs of her eyes. She rose and pummeled the side of the farm stall, but as soon as she saw the wide-mouthed piccanins eying her she left off and resumed her seat.

That evening after supper, she took a torch and went out and scratched with her penknife inside the hearts she had carved on the aloes the initials of herself and Peter Westgate.

This was the headachy, thundery time of summer. Every afternoon clouds crowded the sky and they rumbled and barked, but there was no rain, not even a monkeys' wedding.

The third week presented itself and the days passed leadenly. Edna no longer jumped up when she saw a vehicle on the ridge of Makagabe Hill; and the pain in her side disappeared. A numbness replaced it, filling every inch of her.

On the Wednesday afternoon of the fourth week, she saw the blue-and-white car.

But the timing was cruel, a heartless stroke. It could have happened at any time in the previous weeks, but it had to happen at this minute. For some while she had heard, but hardly registered, the straining sound of the Ford approaching from the west, ploughing through the mogonono sand.

If only she could turn it back!

However, it was too late.

The moment Edna sprang up at the sight of the car racing down Makagabe Hill, that very moment the truck bounded out of the gateway, scattering the piccanins, and bore down on the farm stall in a shower of stones.

Mr. Ferris did not switch off the engine. He clambered out. His tennis clothes stuck to him and his face was moist and gray. He grabbed Edna by the wrists, and she tried to pull away.

"Come quickly," he spluttered. "We need you!"

Edna saw the car half a mile off, on the flat. She struggled, dragging herself away from her father, but he was too powerful, and in seconds he had her in the cabin of the truck and he had stamped his foot on the accelerator, hurling them forward. They roared through the gateway.

By this stage Peter Westgate must have been close to the farm stall, slowing, putting on brakes. Edna looked back, but the thick bush cut off her view.

She wanted to open the door and fling herself out. She battled with the handle. It had jammed. Mr. Ferris leaned across and smacked her hands away. Edna turned angrily on her father. "Have you gone mad?" she shouted. "Where are you taking me? How can you do this to me?"

The truck was touching sixty, far too fast and dangerous for the state of the track. They were in a gray tunnel, the mogonono bushes on either side a blur. Mr. Ferris's knuckles were white from the hard grip he had on the steering wheel.

As soon as the truck had reached the house, she would run back to the farm stall, run back the three miles as fast as she could. Maybe he would still be there, waiting for her.

"What are you up to?"

She saw his rubbery lips moving, but the only word she could read on them was "Gloria."

Elias was prancing agitatedly on the front steps, the red tennis cap bobbing. Sixpence stood solemnly by the headless lion, his racket against his chest as though he was on guard.

Elias left off his jumping up and down and darted out to meet the truck.

"For two hours it has been going on and nothing will come! Gloria is having a baby! Oh, Edna, Edna, help us!" There was true anguish in him; she recognized it.

"It is all because we have been drinking too much," said Sixpence. "And smoking."

"Shut up, you stupid ignorant Kaffir!" boomed Elias, giving Sixpence a shove that almost toppled him.

Mr. Ferris and Elias hustled Edna into the house. She expected to hear screams and groans. She imagined, as they

120

banged through the fly-screen door, Gloria gripping the brass pillars of the bedstead, her back arched like an acrobat's.

There was no sound inside the house, however, only the scraping of their feet on the coir matting as Mr. Ferris and Elias drove her along the passage, to the room that had been Evadne Ferris's. The house was blindingly dark. She would have to get her eyes accustomed to the gloom.

They herded her into the room. A strong smell of ammonia pinched her nostrils. Behind it lurked another smell, a bad one of wild animal skins that had not been properly cured.

Edna made out two forms on the floor, and when her vision came back she saw that one of them was the witch doctor, a grizzled woman who was said to be a hundred years old. The witch lived in a hut on her own, apart from the kraal, with her dried animal organs and bones and powders and crushed insects; and no Native dared go there except on business. Edna could recall having seen the witch only three times in all her life. She had come upon her by accident, as a girl, when she used to wander about the veld. And she had run for her life on each occasion.

The witch was on her haunches in Evadne Ferris's bedroom, her knees jutting above the level of her hunched shoulders. The men must have sent for her because they were desperate. She wore a necklace of porcupine quills and a shawl of monkey tails. They looked like worms coming out of her body. Scattered around her on the floor was her paraphernalia. Edna dared not look at it. "Why is that thing here?" she demanded, pointing.

"Gloria wanted her," said Mr. Ferris. "Oh, don't just stand there, Edna. Do something!"

"What can I do?" He was not being rational. "What do I know about these things?"

"You're a woman, aren't you? Can't you help her? Can't you see she's suffering?" It was Elias who spoke this, crowding up behind her. There was no trace of affectation about him now.

"But I know nothing about babies being born! If you want

magic, you've got the right person over there." The witch had wispy hair plaited with mud. She was making a little cairn of pebbles, dipping her hand into a stained tobacco pouch for them.

Edna collected herself. "Why don't you send for the doctor in the Capital?" she said. "Or Sister Clothilde?"

"What, and let the whole world know? Be sensible, my girlie."

Mr. Ferris was ignored.

"Going for the doctor, that would take six hours!" said Elias. "You've got to do something, Edna, you must. She's dying!"

And for the first time since being thrust into the room, Edna settled her eyes on Gloria.

Her mind went back months and she saw that shiny body again in the water of the moonlight, slithering along the garden paths, with Mr. Ferris drooling after it. She pictured the two of them doing their obscene dance on the tennis court. But, Edna calculated, the child must have been made before that night, before she had discovered what was going on.

Anyway, this was the final result: this woman lying on her back on the floor, on a sheet, in the damp of the liquid that had spurted out of her, her head lolling on a pillow, the eyes turned up so violently that only the whites showed. Gloria was naked now, too, but her body was ugly because of her swollen, pulsing belly. It made her normally thickish legs look spindly. They were sticks. Her chatty-cat was there for everybody to see. Gloria's face was ashen.

Edna spun on her father and said, "See, see what you have done!"

"Now, my girlie, I don't want you climbing up onto a soapbox and telling me what's right and what's wrong."

"No, no," chorused Elias and Sixpence. Sixpence still held the racket, as if at any moment he might have to defend himself. The witch doctor was gathering up her bits and pieces, wagging her head in an affronted way.

Gloria moved slightly and moaned.

"You must help my sister!"

It came as a great surprise, a shock, it was inexplicable, the surge of feeling for Elias that took over Edna. She put out a hand to touch him, but drew it back.

She had seen her white cat giving birth under the kitchen table; she had picked up information here and there in the books she had read. There had also been Evadne Ferris's medical dictionary. That was all she had to go by.

"I'll try," she said.

Edna left the room. She saw the witch, a hoop, rolling along the passage and out the front door.

In the medicine chest in the bathroom was a bottle of castor oil. She pulled it off its shelf. Other bottles were dislodged and they smashed on the floor. Splashes of iodine dyed her legs. From the cupboard she took an armful of towels. Elias and Sixpence were under her feet, asking what they could do, eager to help. "Boil some water," said Edna.

"Find a pair of scissors, sharp ones." They flew about the place.

"Drink this, Gloria," said Edna, holding up the girl's head and pouring castor oil down her throat. She gulped and gasped and struggled like a child. The others held her. "There's a good girl." The last glistening drop disappeared.

Then came a long wait, an anticlimax, when they stood around Gloria, the four of them, watchers, sentinels. The water boiled over in the kitchen.

Night fell. Sixpence brought in the candles, blue packets of them, from the pantry, and stuck them on the floor in beds of wax. The room flickered and smoked. The candles added to the heat, but nobody thought to tell Sixpence to blow them out and bring in the Handigas lamp instead. The candles were part of a ceremony.

Gloria was breathing in grunts. That was the only sound in the stuffy room. Edna gave her water to sip. She longed for the baby to come out. She had never been in the presence of birth. She felt a tremendous involvement. It had the effect of occupying her mind totally, so that there was no longer room for thoughts about Peter Westgate.

After an age, Gloria all at once jerked convulsively, and

her mouth was wide in a soundless cry. Her back formed a bridge between her head and her heels. Sixpence let out a whimper and moved against the wall, in among the shadows.

The bridge of Gloria's back collapsed, but a few seconds later she was rigid again. Then she flipped over so suddenly and so quickly that the three of them, out of alarm, retreated toward where Sixpence stood.

Gloria was crouching on her elbows and knees. Her buttocks moved in spasms. There was something strong and magnificent in the broken rhythms of her body. She was wailing to herself, digging her fingernails into the floor.

The men looked at Edna. "We'll just have to wait," she said, frightened. "It should be coming soon. Fetch the hot water." She had never felt so helpless.

The baby, bound in a caul, like the ballroom dancers in their glass bubble, forced itself out and dropped onto the messy sheet. Gloria gave a tremendous sigh, the sound of the sea changing, and lay on her side, exhausted. Her breathing steadied itself.

Elias and Edna worked together swiftly and silently, by some unexpected inspirational gift now sure of what they were doing, as though they had been through this before, were practiced at it. They pierced the caul and peeled it off, casting the crimpled skin aside. The oval of water that had surrounded the baby broke and spread across the saturated sheet and onto the floor.

They tied two knots and then cut the umbilical cord with the scissors. Edna held the baby by its heels and smacked it sharply, so that it opened its mouth to yell and sucked air into itself and began to live. It spluttered and bleated.

During all this, Sixpence stood stock-still with enormous eyes. Mr. Ferris was marching on the spot, his knees going higher and higher, not moving forward an inch, stuck where he was. His hands were extended, as though he held out an offering, one of the Magi. But soon he was to change.

The baby was raucous now, squirming in her hands, a worm on a hook. Edna saw that it was a boy.

The baby was black.

Drop it this instant, this is your only chance! Let it slip from your grasp—you can say it was an accident; who will be able to prove that it wasn't?—let it fall onto the floor.

The devil was speaking in her head through a megaphone. She wanted to block her ears.

"Here—quickly!" said Edna, holding out the baby to Elias. "Take it!"

"It is not my child," said Mr. Ferris with a groan. "Not mine." Nobody would look at him.

Sixpence lurched out of the room and was sick in the passage.

Elias washed the baby in the basin and Edna cleaned up Gloria. They tossed the soiled towels in a corner. Gloria was singing faintly and drowsily to herself, through dry lips. Edna mopped up the floor.

Then they lifted Gloria and placed her on the bed. They covered her with a clean sheet. Elias put the baby beside her, wrapped in a towel, only its screwed-up face showing. Its eyes were shut, but its face sought blindly, quiveringly, for a nipple. Gloria was fast asleep. However, the baby drank lustily.

"Come, my Dad." But Mr. Ferris would not budge. He was sitting in the armchair beside the brass bed and he said they were to leave him, he wanted to stay where he was, he wanted to keep watch over Gloria.

Elias and Edna left the room. Sixpence was cleaning up in the passage. "It is the smell and my tummy," he explained.

Elias threw his arms around Sixpence. "I am an uncle!" he said, beaming. "Let us celebrate!"

The three of them toasted the new life, Elias and Sixpence with *mampoer* and Edna with orange squash. It did not strike her as odd that she should be with these two men. It seemed to her quite natural that they should be together on the veranda, drinking the health of the baby.

Edna was very tired; a tiredness of immense heaviness was on her, and when she had finished her Oros, she said good night and went to bed.

But Elias and Sixpence kept it up. One of them let Oubaas loose, and the last thing Edna remembered was his clattering on the roof. She had forgotten the evil that had been in her when she had held the baby. She had forgotten, for the time being, Peter Westgate.

Eight

✳✳✳ Edna could tell by the texture of the light that she had waked up later than usual. Stark brightness lay in ripples on the floor. She would have slept longer, except some sound had obtruded. However, as she stirred under the sheet, her ears trying to find out what it was that had broken into her sleep, the house was silent. She listened for Oubaas on the roof, but the baboon had gone.

Then the sound came again: a low moan, rising and falling, whether a man or a woman she could not tell. The moaning was moving along the passage toward her, and she could hear feet shuffling, accompanying the sound, an old person's feet dragging with weariness. The moaning was outside her door; it darkened the room. Edna watched the door handle and, just as it began to turn, she shut her eyes. There was a wave of peach-brandy fumes, and somebody had entered.

"Edna," said Elias in a low voice. "Edna, wake up."

When she opened her eyes, his face was hanging over her, so close that it was out of focus.

But then he stepped back and she could see him properly. He looked dreadful.

She was so accustomed to finding him grinning and bowing and speaking cockily that this new aspect scared her, and she wished it had been the old Elias there, whom she could safely dislike, rather than this spooky person.

A kind of pity took hold of her; she wanted to comfort him, and this was so far out of her reckoning as regards Elias that dismay seized her and her heart raced. "What is it?" she said. "What's gone wrong?" She sat up, clutching the sheet to her chin.

Elias had crumpled to the floor. He was in a heap. Whatever had happened, Edna thought that this was a bit excessive. She was about to tell him to pull himself together when Elias raised his head and said in a cracked voice, pausing between each sentence, "Something terrible has happened. God Almighty has punished us. The baby is dead."

"Dead?" Edna echoed the word. "Dead?" She jumped out of bed, the sheet draped about her. "That's impossible!" She ran along the passage but before she had turned the corner she slowed and began to drag her feet. It was almost as if an outlandish infection were on the house, making everybody in it walk slowly.

At the door to Evadne Ferris's bedroom, before she had touched the porcelain handle with its design of roses, she had the strange notion that Oubaas was responsible for what had occurred: somehow the baboon had got in during the night and had taken the baby's head in his jaws.

Edna opened the door and pushed her way through the heavy stale air between her and the bed. The snuffed candles stood on the floor like stalagmites, and Edna stepped carefully over them.

There were no fang marks on the baby. Its body was wrinkled. It lay discarded at the foot of the bed, on top of the sheet, close to the hump of Gloria's toes, waxy and lifeless.

Edna had never seen a dead person before—it had been one of her dreads—and she had thought she would not be able to bear to look at one. But this baby hardly counted. She had the impression that it was made out of Plasticine. All she had to do was to take it up and squeeze and mold it into a ball, after which the Plasticine could be used to model something else—a cow, a tree, a mushroom, a chameleon. The head had no flesh on it: it was a skull hung with skin. Part of her wanted to take up the dead baby and cradle it, perhaps breathe life into it; but the other part dared not touch it. At length Edna pulled her eyes away from the shape at the foot of the bed and she took in the other two people in the room.

Gloria was propped up on the pillows. Her breasts were taut. She was smoking. There was a long piece of bending ash attached to the end of the cigarette, which Gloria held carefully between the tips of two fingers. She raised it slowly to her lips and sucked at it. The ash broke off and snowed onto the sheet.

Smoke rose from the tip of the cigarette in a straight line, like a pillar, to a certain height, where an air current broke it up. Then Edna noticed that tears had made ruts down Gloria's cheeks; and they continued to come out of her eyes, wetting her face. She was crying silently. She did not seem to be aware that Edna was in the room, and when she did glance at her, it was without interest, as if at a familiar inanimate object. Edna did not like to look at her because of the stunned suffering she saw on her face.

Mr. Ferris, unmoving in the armchair on the far side of the bed, sunk in it, had been regarding Edna closely and suspiciously since she had entered the room. She turned her attention to him now. His eyes were dents in his puffy face, and the bristles on his chin were unruly. His breathing was shallow, as though there was a blockage in his throat and air could go down only so far before being forced back. Their eyes held each other for some while, and then Edna said, "What happened?"

"Why are you all dressed up in a sheet?"

"What happened?" Edna repeated.

Mr. Ferris gave an infinitesimal wag of his head and his little finger jerked, as if to point at the body, but lost its energy and rejoined his hand. "It died."

"I know that," Edna said. Her voice was about to rise, but something inside her checked her. "I thought you were going to keep watch?"

One of Mr. Ferris's eyelids drooped. "I was. But I am afraid I fell asleep. When I woke up, the little thing was dead. Get rid of it for me."

"Get rid of it?"

"Bury it. Far away."

"Doesn't somebody have to sign a death certificate?"

"A lot of useless red tape," said Mr. Ferris, loudly. "I don't see the necessity for a death certificate when it hardly lived at all. The authorities need never know. Nobody need ever know. This will be our secret—yours and mine and Gloria's and Elias's and Sixpence's. It's better that way."

And here Gloria spoke. Her voice was gravelly because of her tears. She did not look at either Mr. Ferris or Edna as she said, "In the night, he smothered it."

"Shut up!" Mr. Ferris exploded angrily, in English. "Stop your sniveling." He dropped his voice and said to Edna, "Don't listen to her. She's out of her mind, half crazy. Now you go and do what I told you."

Edna backed out of the room.

She needed some activity to keep her mind from straying into dangerous quarters where she could not trust her sanity. It was convenient to forget some things that were said.

She busied herself. She went to her room and put on clothes. Elias had gone. She got a shoe box from the storeroom and wiped the dust and the cobwebs off it and made a bed of cotton wool on the bottom. On this she sprinkled some of her scent from Peerbhay Brothers. She painted a cross and a bleeding heart on the lid of the box. She returned to Evadne Ferris's room.

Mr. Ferris was singing in a moldy voice, "O, nobody knows the trouble I've seen . . ." Gloria coughed behind her tears. Neither of them took any notice of Edna.

Before she touched the body, she looked into its face. The eyes were open, staring marbles. They were reddish, as her white cat's had been. She fitted the body into the box, on the cotton wool. Quickly she put on the lid. She was about to close the door when Mr. Ferris broke off his song and said, "Is there any drink left in the house, do you know?" She did not answer him.

She collected a spade from next to the kitchen stove, took the umbrella out of the hall stand and opened it, and stepped out into the day. The shoe box was under her arm. The light was shattering and made her eyes constrict and the nerves in her head pulse. There was a white sky.

The fat blue-headed lizards flicked into the cracks in the stone wall of the graveyard as she approached. The garden gate creaked, and blackjacks stuck to her.

She chose a spot between the two graves. She stood the umbrella on the ground and placed the cardboard box inside the loops of shade. The earth was hard, and the spade clanged against small rocks.

While she was digging, Edna became conscious of somebody watching her; a feeling in her spine told her this. She wheeled round, trapping the piccanin before he had time to duck behind the wall. His skin, she saw, was full of chicken pox and his hair was a leprous gold. It was Cyprian the albino.

Fury rose in Edna. She picked up stones and flung them at the piccanin to chase him off. He did not seem to want to retreat, but when a stone caught him on the head he gave a cry and hopped out of her range. He stood there and waited.

The hole didn't have to be deep, and after the top crust the ground was softer, friable. At two feet, she stopped. She lowered the box into the shallow pit and, kneeling, put her arms around the mound of soil and drew it over the gap. The first grains hit the cardboard like rain. Once the hole had been filled, Edna patted down the hump with the back of the spade. That made three now, under the motseara trees.

She stood up and brushed the knees of her jeans with her knuckles. The business had been so inadequate. She felt that something more was required of her, but she did not know what. A prayer? A prayer would have been ash in her mouth. Neither could she throw herself down on the small patch of broken ground and weep and hug it, the way she had hugged her mother's grave on certain nights and the tears had come like a purge. That would never happen again. She did not belong to the tiny cemetery any more; it gave her nothing.

And yet perhaps a tear or two might help? But her eyes were parched, and she asked herself if she could ever expect to cry over anything again if she could not cry now. She had brought this child into the world. After all, he was in a way part of her; she could not deny that. Then the colder, more organized, more honest side of her brain said that the baby had hardly lived, its life had amounted to a few hours, it was far better that it had died.

She stood like stone under the umbrella, and the lizards poked their heads out of the slits in the wall but, seeing the place still occupied, slid them back again.

Two hundred people had attended Grandpa Ferris's funeral—so she had often been told—coming from all over the Territory to honor the man who had fought the Boers and helped build the railway line and shaken Rhodes and Jameson by the hand. Two hundred people, and there had been a wake afterward that was still talked about.

A voice said right next to her ear, "Where is the child's soul?" This made her go tense, until she realized that the voice belonged to somebody who did not exist. Often birds in the bush called out messages to Edna; and, when she was younger, phantoms had spoken to her.

She began to ransack around, however, for an answer to the question. His soul was with God, naturally, in a place of refreshing coolness, light, and peace. She had got this phrase from the missal with bright silk markers that Sister Clothilde had given her years ago, during the period she had wanted to become a Roman Catholic, had been fervent and holy and excited, planning her life on the lives of the saints she had pored over in a pious book, another gift from the nun. She had wanted to go and work among the lepers in the Congo, or play the harpsichord in a cell, or live in a cave on locusts and honey; or, best of all by far, be martyred. However, Evadne Ferris had spied on Edna through the slot of the keyhole, Edna kneeling on the uncarpeted floor of her room for hours on end, and she had reported this to Mr. Ferris, who in turn drove to the Mission and told Sister Clothilde she was to stop her attempt at conversion at once and that she must not interfere with Edna in this way. So Edna's religious phase was put an end to. Mr. Ferris offered her nothing to replace it. He destroyed the missal.

"The child wasn't baptized." Edna shook her head to try to get rid of the voice. However, it persisted. "He wasn't even baptized." And that meant Limbo. At the Convent, where the non-Catholics had had to remain in the classroom during the religious instruction lessons, she had formed her own ideas of Heaven and Hell and Limbo. Heaven and Hell had color. Limbo was this place, this place she was in now, this vast gray plain of sand, tough grass, aloes, and thorn trees. The child was in Limbo for eternity. He could never get out. His soul would roam these blighted regions for ever and ever. She shuddered.

She shut the squeaky gate and began to walk back to the house, holding the umbrella low, enclosing herself in a black tent, so that she saw only the rutted ground at her feet.

Yet shapes appeared in her mind. There was her mother, her hair hanging to her waist, in the misty distance, beckoning to her; her mother who had been driven to her death. (Forget what you cannot bear. That was an old German proverb. Sister Clothilde had handed it on to her.) Then Brother Martin materialized, smiling nervously, his right eyebrow going up. Edna saw the square diamond-decorated ring of Peter Westgate; and the cuff links with the emperor's bald head.

He would be back in Johannesburg by now!

The events since the previous afternoon had pushed Peter Westgate out of sight. And now that he was trying to come forward, she would not let him. She refused to allow herself to go beyond the ring and the cuff links. She would not let anything else be constructed on that foundation. It would be wisest to forget the man. She would not see him again.

"Missie," said a hissing voice to her left; and she wondered who it was this time, what person who lived in her brain. "Missie Edna," the voice came again, more firmly. She tilted the umbrella and saw, some yards off, Cyprian. She couldn't get rid of him; he was a persistent fly.

Edna took no further notice of the piccanin with the white and red skin of sores, and continued on her way. He moved parallel with her, as if a fence separated them, repeating

"Missie Edna, Missie, Missie." A snake spitting: he was trying some taunting game, but she would not give him the satisfaction of responding.

She went round the back of the house and she let down the umbrella. Squatting on the kitchen steps, a lump of clay, was the old witch. Next to her, like a companion, sat Oubaas, scratching for fleas.

The sight of the two startled Edna. She gave a tiny gasp, and the baboon rose and lumbered toward her. She kept him away by poking at him with the umbrella.

The witch shifted her head. Her yellow eyes were wide open. The sun's glare could not have affected them. The skins she wore made her look like an animal. She told Edna she had come to be paid.

Edna could not answer her. She wanted to get into the safety of the house as quickly as possible; but, when she took a few steps forward, the witch heaved herself up and blocked the way. The old woman said again in her tongue that she wanted money, a pound, two pounds.

Edna turned and hurried round the side of the house to the front. She half expected the witch to be stationed there as well; and when indeed she saw a figure coming down the steps, she cried out.

However, it was Elias.

His head was on one side, resting on the pillow of his shoulder, and he moved lethargically. Edna stood still in the driveway, and Elias came in her direction, lugging his feet. He had on his tennis cap and his head was red again. She thought he would stop and address her, but he went past her, unaware of her presence.

When he had gone some yards beyond her, she called, "Wait a minute, Elias," and she went up to him. His eyes were void. "Where are you going?" He stared at her as if he had not grasped what she had said, and Edna was about to state her question again when his face showed some understanding.

Edna saw two of herself reflected in his eyes. She had never let her gaze settle on Elias for so long. A needle of pity jabbed her. If, however, she had taken time to ask herself whether she was sorry for him, she would have denied—or tried to deny—that she was. Habit had made it difficult, almost inconceivable, that she should ever feel sorry for him. But habit had been turned upside down. She saw and recognized real grief on his face. A mask had been taken off to show something she had never expected to see on Elias. Nevertheless, she knew very well what it was.

She stood in the glass balls of Elias's eyes like two people, tiny, seen through the wrong end of binoculars.

He had heard her. He said, "You ask me, Edna, where I am going?" His tone was flat. "I am going back to Gowani."

"Walking all that way?"

"Sixpence took the buzz-bike. He left at midnight. You will never see me here again."

This last sentence, spoken as if it was of little consequence, unnerved her. It was so irregular, coming from Elias, the Elias whom at one stage she had visualized as the future master of Sherwood Ranch in everything but name. It was as if the man had been turned inside out. "Why?" asked Edna, perplexed.

"Because of all the bad things."

She knew whom this referred to, and she went to the defense of her father. "We can't blame him for everything. We should try to understand why he has become like he is."

Elias shrugged. He blinked once, his eyelids closing and opening, the shutter of a camera. "I know too much."

"What?" Edna had a sinking feeling. "What do you know?"

He was reluctant to admit anything, but she pressed him. "That he killed the baby because it was black?"

"That . . . The baby is dead; there is nothing that can be done now except be sad. In a month we will have forgotten it. Other things."

Edna clasped her hands and lifted them in appeal. "Please tell me."

After a moment or two, Elias said, "About you."

"Me?"

"He will never let you go because . . ." She waited in

fear for what Elias had to say. "Because . . ." But he trailed off again. He switched his track, shifting to something else. After clearing his throat, he said, "One thing I must tell you and that is about your Matric. Your examination papers were never posted. When the father from the Mission brought all the papers to Gowani, I took yours out and burned them. Archie asked me to do that. And I did it. I am sorry."

Whatever Elias had been on the point of revealing when he had cut himself short twice after the word "because," this new piece of information was upsetting enough. Edna felt as if her body was being crushed. She became unconscious of the external world. Then she surfaced, and the vividness of the sun made her head spin. "He would not have done a thing like that!"

"He did." Elias spoke calmly. "I must go now. Tell Gloria I will send for her soon. Good-bye." He was about to put out his hand, but he changed his mind.

Elias turned and plodded down the driveway. The border of upturned bottles glinted. His shirt hung out at the back, flapping a bit. The sole of one of his tennis shoes had come loose at the toe and it flopped in the sand. She always associated him with takkies.

Edna watched Elias until the thorn bushes hid him. He kept his word: as far as she knew, he never came back to Sherwood Ranch.

Edna fetched a hammer.

"Is that you, my girlie?"

"Yes." She was standing outside the door of Evadne Ferris's bedroom, but she did not go in.

They were hungry, Mr. Ferris said, and he wondered if she'd get them something to eat.

It was pointless walking around with the hammer because she would never use it. Her murderous mood swiftly wore itself out. She put the hammer back on the pantry shelf.

She prepared a meal of Post Toasties and rusks and coffee. While she was in the kitchen, she crept to the window and looked out with one eye. Their backs were against the door and she could not see them, but their slanting shadows, inter-mingled, lay on the ground and she knew that the witch and the baboon were still there.

She carried the tray to the bedroom. The air inside it was awful, like that of a cave where dassies and bats live. Mr. Ferris and Gloria were exactly as she had left them. She wondered if Gloria would ever cease crying. There was no indication that any time had intervened since Edna had last been in the room.

She set down the tray. She pulled back the curtains, slid the fly-screen hatches up, and opened the windows. Air, warm but fresh, rushed in. The smell of dried blood was the first to go.

Light whipping into the room made Mr. Ferris flinch and plaster a hand over his eyes. His lips moved. "Did you do what I asked you to, my girlie? Did you bury it?" His voice was a blunt knife on stone.

"The witch doctor is outside," said Edna, ignoring his in-quiry. "She wants to be paid."

He said she would find money in his sports jacket. So she left them and went to his room and opened the cupboard. The moth balls rolled from side to side. She rummaged in the pockets, but there was no money. She fished out a letter and read it. There was fluff in the creases of the paper. It was the one from Evadne Ferris in which she had asked for a divorce.

Something else Edna found in one of the pockets: a flat square tin. There was a picture of a star with a long tail on it, a heavy black comet. She slid out the lid and saw squashed in the tin three powdery rubber slugs. She unrolled one. It was a balloon. She tried blowing it up but the rubber was too tough and flecks of powder left a nasty taste in her mouth. She couldn't fit it back into the tin, so she kicked it under the cupboard.

Then Edna remembered that she herself had money, the pound Elias had paid her at the farm stall. She collected the envelope from the top drawer of her desk, tore it open, and took the pound note to the witch. Edna opened the back door boldly. "Here." The ancient woman's eyes caught fire and she snatched at the money. "Go away now."

Oubaas went with the witch. He followed her like a pet.

Edna returned to Evadne Ferris's bedroom to fetch the tray. At last Gloria's eyes were shut. She and Mr. Ferris were asleep. One of them must have gone across the room in Edna's absence because the curtains were closed once more and the light was murky and heavy. In the armchair, Mr. Ferris snored, the bubbly sound coming from the roof of his mouth. Gloria's breasts were hitched over the top of the sheet. The nipples were still tight. There were cigarette burns on the sheet.

Edna washed up. She could not eat. Her appetite, she imagined, was gone forever. In Evadne Ferris's bedroom, all was silent.

Edna sat out the rest of the day on the veranda; and as soon as the shadows of evening wrapped themselves around the house, she went to bed.

When it was quite dark, somebody scratched, then rapped, on her window; and she heard, muffled through the glass, the piccanin's "Missie, Missie. Missie Edna."

She got up quickly to drive him away but when she reached the window he had already gone. However, on the sill she spotted the envelope, a white block, and she brought it in.

It had a weight in it. The envelope was soiled with finger marks, she noticed when she had lighted the lamp. There was writing on it, the ink smudged by now. "Miss Marguerite de la Hunt," she read. "Per kind favour of Cyprian."

Edna tore open the envelope with eager fingers. Something fell to the floor and rolled under the bed.

Inside was a card, on which was scrawled yesterday's date and these words, "Marguerite—So very sorry to have missed you. I hope I soon have the pleasure of meeting you again. Yours sincerely, Peter Westgate."

Edna's spirits began to rise out of their lowest depths.

She was flustered: her stomach swerved this way and that and her throat dried up.

She would have to be cautious and at all costs not read too much into what he had written.

Her fingers shook as she held the card and went over it again and again. When her mind began to clear, it was the word "soon" that her eye first took up and queried. What precisely did he mean by that? To her, "soon" conveyed tomorrow or at the most next week, nothing later; but to him it might well mean six months' time, when he had said he was next due to travel the Territory.

He was sorry to have missed her; he spoke of pleasure. . . . She examined every word carefully. "Sincerely" rather spoiled the effect: it was too formal.

And yet, she permitted herself to believe, a strong feeling came out of these ordinary words. She counted them: there were twenty-three. He had written her twenty-three words; he cared for her.

Her heart sang, and at the same time the "Toreador Song" struck up, too. She had not heard it for some while; she thought it had deserted her, and she rejoiced at its return. An old friend was back. The music was loud in her head. Edna hugged herself and twirled about. Faster and faster she went, until the room was out of control. She fell onto her bed, her face in the pillow, and let the violent rocking motion subside.

She had not let her emotions stray too far. This time she was sure of herself. The man could fall in love with her. She was convinced of this, not from the point of view of reason but from what she experienced deep down in her core. She herself was in love with him. A gentle, lulling sweetness filled her.

She pulled her head out of the pillow and rolled on her back and smiled into space. She touched her cheek where his hand had rested against it.

She laughed. She hadn't laughed like this since those times in her girlhood when a wild happy mood would overtake her out in the veld and she would throw up her arms and run, her feet flying across the ground, and laugh into the vault of the sky, as she was doing now at the ceiling.

She wanted to dance again, and scrambled off the bed. Then she remembered that something was under the bed, and she got down on her hands and knees and felt for it.

It was a ring, the square gold ring with the P in diamonds.

Edna gasped, and dropped the ring as if it were alive. Straight away she picked it up. Every nerve in her body was alert.

She tried hard to picture what Peter Westgate looked like, but his image evaded her. All that she was able to recall was that he was thin.

He had sent her his ring.

She no longer had anything to fear. The future had come into being again, had been given a meaning; and this time it would not fail her. It was as though all the happiness that she had hounded and that had eluded her for so long had been suddenly presented to her, and at a moment when she had least expected it, when she had given it up for good. For a while she could not cope with this overwhelming feeling, and she felt she was going to be sick. But she remained very still, her knuckles pressed against her teeth, and the nausea passed.

Next she tried on the ring, one finger after the other. But it would fit only her thumb, so she left it there and lifted her hand and pivoted round it, admiring the ring. Her happiness had canceled out all other feelings and she wanted to hurry to Evadne Ferris's room and show it to her father.

But there had been a death in the house. A shadow flung itself across the brightness of her heart. She would have to put her joy in mourning for a while: keep it to herself, hide the ring. At a more convenient stage, she would tell her father. But she wondered, even now, if he would in any way be able to share in her delight.

She put out the Handigas lamp and went to bed, but could not sleep because her brain was far too active. She let her jaw slacken and tried to think of the seaside and the sparkling waves—but tonight this remedy refused to work. She was dashing about huge shops buying furniture and knickknacks for their flat in Johannesburg. Or would it be a house?

She rose and took a blanket and a pillow and the Teddy bear and carted them out of the house to the tennis court, where she lay and watched the stars. A great calm came over her. She kissed every part of the ring; and when at length she dozed, her thumb was in her mouth, like a baby's. There was a dew that night, and she relished its softness and coolness against her skin. No phantoms were wandering about. The mighty space of the veld brought about a sensation that she was, for the moment, the only person in the world.

When the first cocks crowed over by the kraal, Edna went back to the house. With the Teddy bear in her arms, she slept deeply, without dreams.

She woke up happy and she took a bath and while she was in the brown water, she sang. Sing before breakfast, cry before nightfall. So the saying went. Edna dismissed this superstition. However, she wondered, as she lay in the leaf-smelling water, if in singing she was behaving too predictably. She had no guide. There had been nothing like this in her limited experience against which she could measure her feelings. Printed words in a magazine had never dealt with what was in her now. Her body was a garden of flowers and her mind had been cleansed.

Before carrying breakfast to Evadne Ferris's room, Edna was careful to take the ring off her thumb and lock it in the desk. The key she put in the back pocket of her jeans.

She opened a tin of yellow cling peaches and these she gave to Mr. Ferris and Gloria for breakfast, along with Post Toasties.

The room's atmosphere was musty. The chamber pot under the bed was full. Edna did not linger. She put down the tray and said "Good morning," and took in at a glance both her father and the girl. Mr. Ferris might have settled down in the armchair for the remainder of his life. This was the impression his appearance gave. Gloria had come to life a bit. She had her beauty preparations spread on the bed and she was doing something to her hair with tongs and a comb.

Her face had cream on it, a skin whitener, thickly spread, which concealed the tear marks.

It was a relief to get away from the smell of that room.

Edna took the Teddy bear off her bed and dressed it in a new suit and a large pink bow tie with white spots. She would not need the toy again, now that she had the ring. It had served its purpose.

She put up the umbrella. Under it she picked her way through the hot sand to the kraal. Big Mac was slouched against the withered pawpaw tree. There were scraggy bantams at his feet. He glanced curiously at the Teddy bear, which dangled from her hand, and said in a skeptical voice, "They said I must never give you the key again, not after what happened last time."

This reminder of the episode in the "Palace" brought a flush to Edna's face; but as soon as she realized that the whole perspective of her life had altered and that what had happened in the Davidsons' place had lost its value, was no more important than the forgotten entries in the diary she had kept at the Convent, her annoyance with Big Mac left her. (In a way, she was sorry she had not brought him tobacco.) She said, "And I never want to go there again. I have come to look for Cyprian."

Big Mac waved a hand over his shoulder. "He is not here. He is out with the goats."

"Will you give this to him?" She placed the Teddy bear next to Big Mac and he shifted slightly to make room for it. "Tell Cyprian it is a present from me. He will understand."

Edna was walking off and the bantams were clucking rowdily, when Big Mac spoke her name. She turned and faced him. "Yes?" He had removed his head from the trunk of the pawpaw tree and he was looking directly at her with wise eyes. It seemed as if the marble chips cluttering his eyes had grown in size since she had last seen him. Big Mac said, "I hear that they killed the baby." It was as good as a statement of fact; there was no hint of a question in his words.

Edna tightened her grip on the handle of the umbrella. Behind one of the huts, a Kaffir dog began to bark. Big Mac said nothing more, but he kept his cloudy knowing eyes on her, challenging her to deny what he had said. Edna searched helplessly for a reply. A pall was on her.

At length Big Mac took his eyes away from Edna. He flicked a finger against the head of the Teddy bear. It pitched onto its face. She heard the button on its belly give a faint squeak. The barking of the dog had collapsed into a whine.

"It's all right," said Big Mac, wearily. The audience was over. "It doesn't matter." He made a sign to Edna that she could go. And he laid his head against the trunk of the tree and closed his eyes.

While she was on her way back to the house, Edna's feeling of oppression lifted. Her life had changed completely, she told herself; only good things were in store for her now. She had the ring, and Peter Westgate would come back for her. With this knowledge, she could afford to be charitable: she could forgive her father for destroying her examination papers; she could sympathize with him over the deprived life he had been dealt; she could comprehend that he was perhaps incurably lonely. As regards the baby, she shut her mind; in the same way, she had obscured as much as she could her awareness that her mother had killed herself.

That afternoon, Sixpence arrived on the buzz-bike with a message from Elias. Gloria was to be ready at ten the next day, when a taxi would come from the Capital to collect her. Gloria would stay there with an aunt. Later, other arrangements would be made.

"No," said Mr. Ferris. "That won't do. If she must go, I will take her. Are you ready?"

Gloria got up and went to her kia and packed her belongings. These Mr. Ferris stacked on the back of the truck. The Singer sewing machine was a paperweight on top, holding down the accumulations of her life.

When the truck had gone, Edna went out the back way and crossed the yard to the kia. Except for the crowd of pictures on the walls, the room had been stripped. The Queen was there in a ball gown and a politician was showing his teeth. The bed, standing on four bricks, looked like a deserted chicken coop; and all that was left in the cupboard made out of packing cases was the linings of newspapers, their edges cut into frills.

Edna returned to the house. She entered the soiled bedroom and threw open the windows. She spent hours cleaning the place out. She washed down the walls and scrubbed the floor.

She was alone in the house that night, but she had her ring to keep away evil.

Mr. Ferris came back at noon the following day, and she went out into the heat to meet him. His face was blotched: white from having been indoors for a number of days, the color of an insect that lives under a rock; and red from the drinks he must have poured down his throat last night in the Capital.

"Hello, my girlie." He looked harassed. "The rats are leaving the sinking ship—but you are still here. I've still got my own good girlie, haven't I?"

Edna offered no reply. Evadne Ferris had gone, Elias had gone, Gloria had gone, even the baboon had gone. Gradually the house had emptied itself until there were only herself and her father left. But in time, she, too, would be gone. "Soon." Soon Peter Westgate would appear and take her away.

Edna smiled at her father and the creases left his face. He walked jauntily to the truck and lifted out a box. "Look," he said. "I've bought us provisions. Lots of tins of Viennas. And I gave Gloria some boiled sweets."

That afternoon Edna flipped over the leaves of the calendar on her desk and ringed in red a date six months ahead. By then, given the widest margin, Peter Westgate was bound to have returned. That day was the farthest limit, and until it came around she would not think of despairing.

The true problem was how to get across the chasm of time that stretched between now and then. She made up her mind to do the best she could. After all, her life on Sherwood Ranch was no longer permanent, and knowing this would be a help in killing the days and weeks that lay ahead.

Mr. Ferris knocked on the door and suggested tennis. "There's an hour before the sun sets. I know you haven't played for a long time, but won't you today, please, for my sake?"

Her racket had been destroyed, was draped on a thorn tree; however, Elias had left his behind. "It's immaterial to me," said Edna.

They played two sets. Mr. Ferris puffed and wheezed. Edna could have beaten him, but she let him win. Afterward, she entered the date and the scores in the black book. There was nobody to serve the drinks, so Edna brought them out. She wound up the fancy bottle.

A couple of days later, when she raised the matter of the farm stall and said she should be getting back to it, Mr. Ferris's forehead became shiny and he grew agitated. "No," he said. "No, that won't do. It was a total failure, and we'd better cut our losses while we can."

Before she had a chance to say anything further, he ran to the garage and climbed into the truck and drove off. Half an hour later, he was back, with the paraffin fridge, the Primus stove, the table and chairs, and the umbrella.

That night, Mr. Ferris said, "Let me explain. I can't have you out there on the main road running a café any more because I need you to help with the digging."

"The digging?" said Edna. "This is something new."

"Well, as a matter of fact," Mr. Ferris blustered on, "I've been doing some thinking lately, and I believe that you might bring me luck if you came with me. You never know."

She had to hold back a laugh.

However, Edna accompanied Mr. Ferris when he set out westward in the truck early each morning, after coffee and rusks. They took tea with them in bottles. She sat under the umbrella on the bank of the dry spruit with a swatter to keep down the flies. When the sight of their crushed bodies became ugly, she covered them by kicking sand on them.

Edna was bored, but she was also, in a way, content. At least some time was being taken up.

Mr. Ferris had a gang of five Natives from the kraal who

worked under him. He marched up and down the riverbed, carrying a stick like a water diviner. This he would prod periodically into the sand and tell the men, "Dig here." The area was scarred with shallow pits. The men were languid in their work and they joked a lot among themselves, but Mr. Ferris was serious. When they broke into laughter, he scowled.

He grew possessive. Before long it became apparent to Edna that her father did not want her far from his side. He kept her within his sight all day and he would give her up only when it was time for bed. He never saw the ring. She had decided not to tell him about it. She kept it locked up and she would take it out at night, when she was alone, and wear it on her thumb.

The thought struck her out of the blue that when Peter Westgate did come back he would find the farm stall shut up and maybe falling to pieces and there would be no piccanins hanging about to tell him where she was or to carry a message for him. Perhaps he would think she had left the Territory or that she did not care for him. Why hadn't this occurred to her before? Panic streaked through her. What if he returned tomorrow?

"Good night, my girlie, it's been a long day." Mr. Ferris tried to hold her when he kissed her, but Edna wriggled free.

After her father had left the veranda, yawning widely, she gave him five minutes, and then she collected a tin of white paint and a brush from the storeroom. She walked to the farm stall, singing loudly to chase away any leopards there might be lurking in the darkness and stamping her feet to warn snakes she was coming. The only light was from the torch.

On the door of the farm stall, she painted, making the letters as small as possible so as not to attract the attention of anybody passing by: PETER I AM AT THE HOUSE. THREE MILES. COME. And she fashioned a white arrow pointing to the stone gateway to show him the direction.

As she trudged homeward through the still, silent mogonono bushes, Edna felt that she was entering the concluding phase of her life on Sherwood Ranch. Her destiny had finally been decided. She saw the end ahead more clearly than she ever had before. In a while, there would be only her father left.

A light speared the landscape to the northeast. Edna heard the passenger train making its muffled charge through the night. Her soul was on it! She was going at last! Then the brakes caused the wheels of the train to wail as it slowed for its 2:00 A.M. stop at Gowani Siding to take on water.

Nine

✳✳✳ Once again the days lost their continuity. There were no landmarks to distinguish one from the other, and they became blurred. The nights were a few degrees cooler, and in the mornings there was a brief period when the air had a tang in it. Autumn, the season Edna liked best, was on its way. But at noon the sun was as strong as ever. A warm wind nagged the trees for their leaves. In the evenings there was tantalizing sheet lightning in the distance and, on occasion, thunder, a belly sound.

Sixpence kept up the Wednesday tennis and he stayed on for *mampoer* and a meal. He had bought the buzz-bike and had been promoted to assistant postmaster in Elias's place. He told them that Elias had got his transfer to the Capital and that Gloria was working in the kitchen of the Commercial Hotel. The brother and sister shared a room in their aunt's house.

Peter Westgate came back much sooner than six months.

It was at Easter, which was late that year, three weeks before her nineteenth birthday, that the blue-and-white car drove up to the farmhouse. They had not gone out digging because it was Good Friday. The day before, Mr. Ferris had picked up the post at Gowani, and there was a novel from the book club. He and Edna were reading their quota of twenty pages when the car approached. It came so quietly and smoothly that Edna heard it only at the last moment.

"Why—visitors!" said Mr. Ferris, jumping up. "Who can this be?"

The sight of the car jarred Edna so much that for a minute she lost her senses. She rose, scattering the pages of the book from her lap, and fled into the house. Her immediate reaction was to hide somewhere, under her bed or behind the boxes in the storeroom. But halfway down the passage she stopped in her flight and put her hands to her burning cheeks and told herself not to be ridiculous. No harm could come to her.

As she made her way back to the veranda, she began to tremble and go hot and cold.

Her father was greeting the man genially. He had gone down the steps with an outstretched hand, saying, "Come in, come in. This is indeed a pleasure." Edna hung back on the veranda, desperately trying to control her shaking. Her stomach was topsy-turvy.

The slapping of the fly-screen door told her that the men had come onto the veranda, and she heard her father saying, "This is Edna, my one and only daughter."

"Edna?"

Edna raised her head. She was not able to take in much at first, only his lean face with the smile scrawled across it and the fact that he was wearing a white open-necked shirt. She did not trust her voice, but she had to speak, and she said, "Oh, good afternoon. Isn't Fred with you?" As soon as she could, she would take him aside and explain about the Marguerite business. How childish she had been to pretend that that was her name. The memory made her blush.

"Take a pew. This one's guaranteed to be safe."

"Thank you, Mr. de la Hunt."

Mr. Ferris frowned. "De la Hunt? Where did you get that from? The name's Ferris—Archie Ferris."

Edna stepped forward and said in a high, forced, and rather brittle voice, "I thought you said, Mr. Westgate, that you only come round these parts once every six months." She turned to her father. "Dad, Mr. Westgate is a traveler in medical goods."

Mr. Ferris's eyes moved from Edna to the man. "Westgate?" he said, as though the name were fictitious. His voice was cold. Instantly the atmosphere changed as the friendliness drained out of him.

"Yes," replied the man. "Peter Westgate."

There was a scary pause, and Edna felt her blood racing and she heard in her head the sound of drums, heralding a battle, or at least a struggle. She was ready for it, however: this time she would not surrender but would fight.

"So," said Mr. Ferris, letting his hands fall on his knees. He must have summed up quite a bit of the situation. "So you two know each other already?" Anybody could have picked out the hostility in his tone, but it was only Edna who could detect what a strain he was under. A muscle in his cheek twitched. To a stranger this might have appeared to be something habitual, but Edna knew better. It did not often occur, and to her the jerking skin was a danger signal. "Mr. Westgate," she explained as evenly as she was able, "called at the farm stall some weeks back for a glass of milk."

"A glass of milk, did he, how very nice." Then Mr. Ferris said loudly, declaring his position, "So, what's that got to do with his being here now?"

Edna had never anticipated such a violent reaction. She wished she had the courage to reply to her father, but her nerve was in pieces. She doubted, too, if she would have been able to give an accurate answer. If she said that he had come for her, to take her away, it was possible that Peter Westgate as well as her father might have been thrown into amazement. And she could not risk a declaration like that just yet for fear of jeopardizing herself.

Peter Westgate remained unruffled, though he must have been aware of the strong currents of emotion that had been let loose, the eruption his arrival had caused. "It's the Easter weekend," he said. "I have a break, so I thought I'd pay a visit to the Territory, a sort of holiday."

"A holiday? Anybody who comes here for a holiday must be stark raving mad."

"It has its attractions." It was at a later stage, after she had had an opportunity to study this remark for a while, that Edna permitted herself to believe without a doubt that it was she he had come for. However, for the moment, what was taking place in front of her demanded her attention.

"Well, you can't stay here," said Mr. Ferris angrily. "There's no room. The house is full."

"Dad, *please*." Everything was out of alignment. She could find no convincing explanation for the way he was behaving.

"To rely on your hospitality was not my intention." Peter Westgate's voice was as frigid as his words were formal. This told Edna that he, too, was angry, but he kept his anger within bounds. "I came in at the border post in the north and I have booked a room at the Commercial Hotel in the Capital. There is a dance there tomorrow night, and I drove down here to ask . . . Edna, that's it, to ask Edna if she will come to it with me."

"So it's 'Edna,' is it?" He sounded womanish, spiteful, the way Evadne Ferris was in an argument. "I am afraid that that is utterly out of the question. My daughter does not go gallivanting around with every Tom, Dick, and Harry. Neither does she dance."

"Maybe," said Peter Westgate, evenly, "maybe Edna"— this time he did not stumble on her name— "can answer for herself."

She realized that this was the moment of decision. The course of her life was about to be set once and for all. She could no longer afford to hesitate. She knew with an intense certainty that if she wavered now, that would be the end of her. She would spend all the years to come on the farm with her father, condemned to continue her gray existence. Her choice had been presented to her in simple terms, and she knew what to do.

"Thank you very much," she said. "I'd love to come."

She had put a match to a fuse. Mr. Ferris crashed his fist into the fly screen, ripping it open. "I forbid it!" he shouted in a rage. "I absolutely forbid it! You are not yet nineteeen and you will obey your father."

She turned slowly and faced him. His eyes were bulging. "My Dad, it's no good."

There was a knocking sound in his throat. His knuckles

but that's grossly unfair. Stick to the point and don't you provoke me. You know what a temper I've got when I'm roused."

She smiled fractionally. "I know," she said. "I know you only too well by now, my Dad."

Mr. Ferris asserted himself. "If that young man comes sniffing round here tomorrow, I'll greet him with my shotgun."

"You wouldn't dare do anything like that. You are a coward." The words were thorns in her mouth.

Mr. Ferris gaped. "Has it come to this?" he said, tragically. "That I must stand here and listen to my own daughter call me that?" His eyes drooped. "What, I ask God, have I done to deserve this?"

Edna was quick to cut off such a line of approach. "Self-pity isn't going to help you," she said. "I know all your tricks. You can't expect my sympathy any more because it's all gone." She sprung the question at him. "Why did you have my exam papers destroyed?"

"What?" exclaimed Mr. Ferris in disbelief.

"Elias told me."

"Elias lied."

"I believe him. Why must you wriggle out of everything?"

"You would take his word against your father's? Where is my young, innocent girlie? Overnight you have become a hard, cruel woman. Why? If you'd only tell me why, perhaps I could begin to understand." He wiped his swaddled knuckles across his eyes.

"Listen," said Edna. "Listen to what I have to say. Just a few months ago I decided to give up all my dreams of leaving here; I resigned myself to this dreadful world. My life was emptier than it had ever been. And then, one day, a miracle happened! Yes, a miracle—I will call it that. Peter Westgate had a puncture outside the farm stall and he said he liked me, that I was a funny girl. Now he has come back and asked me to the dance. And I will be going."

"Oh, how absolutely bloody marvelously romantic! You have no idea what he's after, have you? You have no notion.

I know his type. I've seen them. I can smell them out a mile off. All he wants from you is what you've got down there. There, in your pants."

Edna turned pale. She thought in some confusion for a moment and then she said, "If that is what he wants, I'll let him have it." She did not give the words time to settle before she added, "You see—I love him."

Mr. Ferris began to wheeze. For some seconds, he grappled with what she had said. "That's a fine one. You 'love' him. How little you know about this world. Life isn't a fairy tale. And I suppose you think he loves you?"

She hesitated, as a gambler might do who is down to his last coin. "Yes," she said at length. "I believe he does."

"Well, let me put you right before you lose all your common sense, let me pull the stars out of your eyes, no holds barred. That gentleman has come here for a dirty weekend, nothing more. He knows a whore when he sees one. He'll take you to the Commercial Hotel and he'll stuff you silly and then he'll drop you."

There was a thumping in the back of her head. She could have thrown Gloria at him. "You can't desecrate what I have found," she said. "He has come hundreds of miles from Johannesburg and he is prepared to drive here three times all the way from the Capital into the bargain. He is doing that because he likes me. Because he loves me. You can't get me all upset; there's no use trying. I know it in my bones that he loves me. You can't call me a whore." She struggled to stop herself from crying. Tears would have been a sign of weakening, and Mr. Ferris would have latched on to that.

"In your bones, do you? So you feel it in your bones? Edna, you're mad. Insane. I presume you also believe that he will propose to you and that you'll live happily ever afterward. Come on—answer me."

After a brief pause, she replied with a question of her own, "Is it so terrible to believe in what you have just said?"

"Shut up!" he shouted suddenly.

She raised her voice, too, to meet his. "Don't bully me! I won't have you bullying me."

This outburst on her part made Mr. Ferris subside a bit. He said, "I just want to make one thing clear: that when and if your admirer pitches up tomorrow, I'll be waiting with my shotgun." He revolved his thumbs round each other and studied them. "Nevertheless, I very much doubt—in my bones—that he will appear."

"If you doubt it, then why are you carrying on like this?"

"It's not me who's carrying on, it's you."

"If you believe he won't come, you have nothing to be afraid of."

"It's because . . ." She had caught him unawares and he had begun to speak before he could pull himself short. "Because," he went on, "I cannot lose you, my girlie. Wait." He lifted a hand. "Don't accuse me again of looking for sympathy but let me have my say, hear me out. I need you here, Edna; you must know that. I'll say it myself. I'll be frank." He paced away from her and then came back. "I won't pretend any longer. Yes, I begged Elias to burn your papers, I'll admit that. When my marriage with your stepmother started going wrong, I took you out of the Convent so that I could have you with me. Is that awful? What would I be if you were to go? They have all gone and left me—except my own girlie. Am I that bad, that everybody must run away from me?"

She led her eyes away from him because she feared the look on his face. On it she saw helplessness, and she did not trust herself not to weaken.

Edna said, "You can't keep me a prisoner."

She heard an intake of breath and she felt him move closer to her. "Look at me, my girlie. Why don't you look at me? Do you want me to go down on my knees and beg you to stay? Do you want me to grovel like that?"

He was at her feet. Edna glanced down at him. She saw the bald patch on the top of his head, a tonsure. "Get up," she said, harshly.

He rose. "You have made me humiliate myself," he muttered.

Her throat and hands were dry. Over the Transvaal, where during the course of the afternoon clouds had been massing, thunder grumbled. Her head was aching dully, as it did when there was thunder in the sky. "At any rate," she said, "in a normal house a father would let his daughter go to a dance."

Mr. Ferris's expression changed. His face was red. "Go!" he exploded. "Go to the dance. What do I care? But don't come running back to me when it's all over. Don't say I didn't do my duty and warn you. Go!"

Edna kept her voice even, patching up the cracks by speaking slowly. "Yes—I will go."

The subject was the dance, but each knew that this was only a term of reference, that what they were in fact discussing was her leaving the farm.

Cornered, Mr. Ferris played his last card. He came out with, "I'll burn the house down. I'll kill myself. I'll hang myself from one of the motseara trees."

Edna wavered for a split second before she said, "Then burn the house down."

Mr. Ferris was aghast. "What did you say?"

"I said it would be better, then, if you did burn the house down. Threats won't work. Neither will bluff."

"Do you mean to stand there," he said, his voice spiraling, "and tell me you don't care if your father commits suicide?"

On the tip of her tongue were the words, "My mother did!" But she stopped them in time. Edna said, "I was talking about your burning the house down."

Mr. Ferris's look of horror doubled. He was at a loss what to reply; but after a while his face rearranged itself, his mouth going hard, and he nodded and said, "Very well, if that's your attitude, then I will."

He left her and went barging into the house.

Edna sat in a grass chair and let go a long sigh.

She had staked everything on Peter Westgate. She did not consider this as a reckless move. He had not only given her the ring and asked her to the dance. It went far deeper than that, in her estimation. What he had done was to offer to share his life with her. She could not have explained to herself why she was so certain this was so. She simply felt the truth of it with her whole being. Her feelings on this point were incapable of deceiving her. Her life had been directed to this crossroads and she knew without a doubt which way to take. She had groped blindly for years; she had been in despair. But that was over.

However, her father's reaction had tarnished her happiness. Over the past six months, her love for her father had dwindled a great deal, but it had not been completely destroyed. Nor could it ever be. (He would come and visit them once a year, for a fortnight, and she would take him to the cinemas. There would be a room set aside for him in their flat or house.)

But, to complicate matters, along with the lees of love that remained in her, there was a deposit of hate. She could not ignore this. Certain events had given her the capacity to hate him.

A roll of thunder came close, crossing the border, the banging of a corrugated-iron sheet with a lead pipe, and made Edna start. She looked to the mountain of clouds in the east and saw that they had grown blacker and had moved in much nearer. They towered above her and gave the impression that at any instant they might topple. Where the slanting sun caught the tops was snow. Way up there, she saw a chalet and flowers and a girl with blond plaits driving a flock of sheep to safety.

A hot high wind had risen, too, and it raked the thorn trees and the scrub, making them crackle. Dust was thick in the air.

At her back, Edna heard the twang of the sides of a paraffin tin as the liquid sloshed against them. Mr. Ferris was moving about the house, sprinkling the rooms with paraffin.

In due course he emerged onto the veranda, where he scattered the last drops from the tin. Edna chose to take no notice. Her eyes were on the spears of vivid lightning that cut into the black mountain. The girl and the snow had gone.

"I am ready now," said Mr. Ferris. "To burn the house down." Edna removed her gaze from the jostling clouds and put it on her father. "This is your last chance," he said, petulantly.

She got up and crossed over to him. Out of the back pocket

of her jeans, she took a box of matches, which she handed to him. "Here," she said.

"Thank you." He took the box; there was nothing else he could do. It was cradled in his hand and he stared at it as if it was something rare and strange.

"Go on," said Edna. "Go on. Strike one."

He waited for a long while, his body swaying slightly, as though the box of matches had mesmerized him. Then Mr. Ferris crushed the box with his fingers. The wood splintered. He opened his hand and tipped the matches onto the stoep like fiddlesticks. He had to search for his voice. It came out a croak. "You are heartless, Edna," he said. "Like all women, you are heartless."

She was aware that she had struck fatally at his dignity and his pride, but she refused to say anything to release him from what he must have been experiencing. She would not allow him a way out. The end of the struggle was in sight, and if she dared give way now, she might be back where she had been, ensnared. She was sorry for him—yes—but she could not relent. She was almost out of his net and she had to beware of making one false move that would give him the opportunity of casting it over her again.

By now Mr. Ferris had seen that he had lost. His face had a filleted look, one of dismal acceptance. His lips were floppy and his eyes were shrouded. Their lids were rubber bands. Edna could not bear to look at him.

She kept her eyes on the granolithic floor. Cracks had made a pattern like a star. Then she saw his sandals down there and the gray socks, and she realized he was right up against her. She felt the tickle of his breath on her neck, followed by the touch of his hands. They moved gently down her bare arms.

She made no effort to pull away when he lifted her chin and put his mouth on hers. It stuck there hungrily, feeding. The bristles in his skin scratched her. His mouth was wet and flabby and open.

Edna was a rag doll in his arms. He had his arms about her now, squashing the breath out of her. She was horrified, on the point of being sick from the shock of what he was doing. But she could not move.

A missing piece fell into place and she saw distinctly, in a flash as clear and sharp and vicious as the lightning that was almost continuous now in the boiling sky, how great a danger he and she would be in if she stayed a day longer.

They would lose their salvation and the farm would turn from Limbo into Hell.

There had been glimmerings before, but their meaning had evaded Edna. Elias had hinted at something. Now the full knowledge came to her, and she was appalled and dumbstruck.

She stayed limp in his arms, and at length he pulled his mouth away.

He let go of her, and a sob came out of him, from his very depths. He moved away from her swiftly and he banged through the fly-screen door and clattered down the front steps. A dust devil, rising out of the driveway, took him and hid him, escorting him round the side of the house as he ran away.

Edna did not call him back. Nor did she go after him. She did not fear that he might be making for the motseara trees to hang himself.

She was in distress. She sat down and tried to put a label on what had just taken place. But she was not given much time.

The Volkswagen arrived. She had not heard it because of the thick thunder. The mountain had broken up and the clouds were washing over the farm, bringing about an eerie twilight, an eclipse. The cocks at the kraal were crowing and birds were making for their nests.

Seeing Father O'Leary coming up the steps, driven by the wind, made Edna consider the odd way events had of withholding themselves for months and then packing themselves into one day.

There was no fun on the priest's face. The crucifix round his neck swung like a pendulum. He greeted Edna brusquely and said, "Brother Martin has run away again and I want to know if you are hiding him."

"Hiding Brother Martin? Me?"

"Don't sound so surprised, Edna. You did once before."

"Where did you get that from? Did he tell you?"

"Never mind who told me. The Territory holds no secrets, least of all from me. Where is he?"

"I am telling you the truth, I really don't know." She should have left it at that, but she added, "If he wants to go, why must you hold him back? Why—oh, why—can't people let others be free?"

Father O'Leary's lips tightened, but he pretended to be deaf to what Edna had said. He sniffed. "What is that most peculiar smell?"

"Paraffin," replied Edna. "There's paraffin all over the place. My father was going to burn the house down but he changed his mind."

Father O'Leary gave her a withering look and snorted. "I can see I'm going to get no sense out of you this afternoon, Edna."

The small red car jolted into the mogonono bushes and as soon as it was out of sight, Edna left the house and headed for the "Palace." She had vowed not to go there again, but this was an emergency.

In the open, her distress lifted and vanished. The air was cool and, though the thunder had multiplied, her headache had disappeared. She ran most of the way. A herd of impala was in her path, just beyond the stile. When they saw her coming, the buck leaped away, soaring above the scrub and aloes and bushes, above the thorn trees themselves, creatures in effortless flight. She held her breath with wonder at the sight. It never failed to astonish her. But now, as she watched the delicate buck flowing through the air, like water, for the first time she was able to imagine herself in their place, free of all bonds, rising with them, floating over the thorn trees, away, away.

When she reached the "Palace," she went round it, knocking on all the windows and calling above the wind, "Brother Martin, are you there? It's me—Edna Ferris."

The Venetian blinds sealed off the inside of the house,

but she could sense there was nobody there. She had not really expected that Brother Martin would make for the "Palace" a second time, but there had been the chance. Wherever he was, she would have liked to be with him for a while, to be able to help him, to be able to communicate to him some of the great sense of freedom that had come to her.

She turned her back on the house. The wind was behind her and it shunted her along. The clouds made an immense black flapping tent. The thorn trees creaked and the thunder banged. The world was full of a wild rushing noise. A bolt of lightning smacked onto the ground and raced haphazardly along the backs of rocks, a snake on fire.

Edna had never known a storm to build up so quickly and ferociously. The unusualness of it exhilarated her. She abandoned herself to it, letting herself be carried like a leaf whichever way the wind veered. She made herself a part of the storm. She shouted at the top of her voice, "I love him! I love him!" But the din of the wind and the thunder and the whining trees swallowed the sound. She let her arms rise from her side as she whirled across the veld.

Edna was on the edge of the landing strip, where the grass hummed, when a giant cloud opened itself and chucked down its rain. The drought had lasted for seven years and it was over. Immediately, the scent of the veld became moist and sweet. She raised her face, as though she were a flower, to receive the raindrops. They stung her, needles against the skin, but she relished them. She laughed and held her arms up, ready to take the rain to her.

The rain fell in a block. It was a downpour such as she had only heard spoken about from other people's memories. For many minutes she could see nothing. Water rose and slapped around her ankles. Then the storm let up a little, clearing, and some hail dropped out of the sky, moth balls that bounced high when they struck the ground. They melted fast.

After this, the rain settled down to a steady pounding fall. Edna was so filled with delight that she stripped off her clothes and danced in the rain.

She went round and round in a dizzying waltz.

She saw, behind the curtain of rain, her father's head in a bush, staring at her, and she stopped at once. His face spun about her until her balance was restored—and then the peering face was gone.

The bush was empty; there was nobody there.

A chill entered her. Hastily, she pulled on her clothes. The face had spoiled everything.

She decided to return to the house straight away, but when she reached the spruit she found that it was in flood.

Most of her life the river had been nothing but dry coarse sand and baked pats of cow dung. The sight of it now, filled with charging brown water, its steep banks crumbling under the force of the torrent, was so unfamiliar that Edna thought for a moment that she had strayed somehow into an unknown country. But just then a shaft of light poked through the clouds and caught the roof of the house, half a mile away; and she knew where she was.

The body of a drowned cow tumbled past her on the waves. The surface of the water was dotted with spinning, diving thorn trees that had been uprooted.

The spruit was not wide—perhaps ten yards—and it was no obstacle to Edna. She jumped in and began to swim to the other side.

But she had reckoned without the secret force of the water. It snatched her up and carried her away.

She did not panic, to begin with.

There was something so relaxing in bobbing along that she simply accepted the river's clutch and pictured herself being carried right across Africa to the Indian Ocean.

Then the trunk of a tree caught her on the back of the head, a cracking blow, and for some seconds she lost consciousness and went under.

When she surfaced, her lungs were filled with water and, in spluttering for air, she gulped in more of the river.

Only then did the possibility of drowning enter her mind, but it seemed so incongruous—to drown in this parched, dry

163

land was a form of death she had never considered—that it was difficult to accept.

However, she was dragged under again into the warm bubbling insides of the river. Her mother beckoned to her.

A beautiful drowsiness was taking hold of Edna and she was ready to give herself over to sleep, as though it were the only thing in the world that mattered, when her brain, in a final burst, began to function and told her that it would be absurd if she were to allow herself to die now, at this vital stage, when her life had at last made its turning.

Peter Westgate was coming for her at three tomorrow afternoon and she had to be there to meet him.

She had to get out. Vainly, Edna struggled to free herself from the grip of the water. Her limbs were weak, and every time she opened her mouth, gasping for air, a wave hit into it. If she had had the strength, she would have given one great cry for help; but that would have been useless because the likelihood of anybody being about to hear her was so remote.

However, there was somebody.

She bumped against the far bank and the mud coated her like slime. And then two hands had grasped the back of her shirt and were heaving her out. She heard and felt the material rip and she expected to be cast into the river again; but the hands held on, and she was pulled from the water.

The river had blinded her. She could see nothing; there were weeds in her eyes. Her cheek rested in slush and somebody heavy was on her back, pushing down her ribs so that the vile water spurted out of her mouth. Clean air was pumped into her lungs.

After a while, she was vaguely aware of being lifted up and carried off.

"It's all right, my girlie." The voice came from a thousand miles away.

Edna remembered nothing more until, some hours later, she came to in her bed in her room. It was nighttime. She sat up, and water dribbled out of her nose. The room was in darkness but she groped for the matches on the bedside table and lighted the Handigas lamp. The room was given a warm, safe glow.

She was naked under the blanket. He had undressed her. She got up and put on her gown and went to find him, to thank him for saving her life.

The house was deserted. She searched for her father everywhere, but found no trace of him. A slight rain still fell, pattering softly on the roof. She stood at the kitchen door and the rays of the lamp spread over the shallow lake that the back yard had become. "Dad, Dad?" she called into the night. There was no reply.

Edna sat in the kitchen and drank coffee from a mug, listening to the rain caress the roof.

What he had done when he had put his mouth on hers, he had atoned for. The leering face in the bush that had etched itself on her mind began to grow dim.

A balm washed over Edna. She was serene.

She sneezed twice. "Once for a wish, two for a kiss."

The sound of the rain lulled her and her head fell lower and lower in little jerks until her chin was tucked into her throat. She made an effort, rose, and returned to her room. She opened the desk drawer and got out the ring. She fell into bed and was instantly in a heavy sleep, the ring hooked on her thumb.

The next day was brilliant. The rain had transformed the world, and there was no feeling of decay. The air was sparkling and the veld clean. The dust of so many years had been settled.

Edna stood at her bedroom window and took it all in. The trees were tinged with green. The paint on the trunks of the ones in the garden had run, staining the ground. The colors of the birds swooping for insects stood out boldly. Near the earth dam was a shimmering cloud of white and green rain butterflies that would live for a day in glory. They were a breath of beauty to Edna.

The sun was climbing slowly and benignly into a blue sky. The thirst of the veld had been quenched for a while, the drought broken. In parts, a delicate smoky mist rose from the ground, wispy. Sounds carried far in the clear air. The birds were raucous, and beyond their notes she heard the spruit, not violent any longer but gurgling, and over by the kraal somebody chopping wood, the ax singing.

Some lines, stored in her memory during her Convent days and neglected, came all at once to her:

> Blessed is the corpse that the rain falls on;
> Blessed is the bride that the sun shines on.

These words caused a surge of gladness in her, and she hugged herself. Some water tumbled out of her nose, and she wiped it on the sleeve of her gown.

Her father? He must have come in during the night. Edna went to look for him. His bed had not been slept in. The room had a desolateness about it, as if nobody would ever use it again, as if it had finished with inhabitants. She went about the house searching for him, opening the doors of all the rooms and glancing in and calling him.

Last night's lake in the back yard had seeped into the ground, but muddy pools were left here and there, in dents, and ducks and pigs splashed in them. Mud oozed between her toes as she crossed the yard. He was not in the shed or the garage or Gloria's kia.

Edna had a mild prick of alarm, but the notion that he might have carried out his threat and was hanging from the branch of a tree in the veld was preposterous, and she threw it out. She knew her father too well. He would be back.

She left a trail of chocolate footprints across the floor. There was still a slight smell of paraffin throughout the house.

She decided she had better eat, so she fried an egg and opened a tin of Vienna sausages; but one thought of Peter Westgate took her appetite clear away, and after a mouthful she put down her knife and fork and pushed aside the plate.

She listened to her body. There seemed to be tiny, jumpy objects inside her: mice running excitedly around her stomach.

She dared not go and look at the grandfather clock in the hall for fear that the time would be much earlier than she hoped it was. At least it was daylight, and it was consoling that the hands of the clock could only move forward.

There was nothing else to do, no matter what the time really was, so Edna decided to get ready for three o'clock.

She hung her gown over the crack in the bathroom door. Tadpoles squirted out of the tap with the water and she scooped them up with the strainer.

This would be her last bath in this ugly room.

In the cupboard was the bottle of mauve bath salts that Edna had been hoarding for a special occasion since her sixteenth birthday. Without hesitating, she undid the mauve bow and pulled out the frosted glass stopper. She poured all the salts into the bath and jiggled the water with her hands until the crystals had dissolved. The salts had gone off and they made a scum. The bath wobbled on its claws when Edna stepped into the reeking water. Two wasps swept out of their nest on the ceiling.

It was only now, as she lay back in the bath, making the plastic fish swim by prodding it with her foot, that Edna realized two things: first, that she could not dance (except the waltz, after a fashion); second, that she had nothing to wear. Why she hadn't considered this before, the moment Peter Westgate had asked her to the dance, she did not know. Frustration nibbled at her.

Her bath was spoiled, the luxury of the salts wasted. She got out and dried herself.

Having nothing to wear was worse than not being able to dance. She should never have cut up her two dresses and burned them; in those dark days, she should have held on to a shred of hope that the time might yet come when she would need them again.

Then Edna remembered the leather trunk in the storeroom. When she was younger, the trunk had been a magic casket, a source of entertainment to her, and she had dressed herself up in what it contained and paraded around the house. However, she could not now recall exactly what was in the trunk. Maybe there would be something just right.

She hurried to the storeroom, but she knew at her first peep, once she had lifted the yellowed pages of newspaper that covered the contents, that the trunk was hardly likely to provide a solution.

Like a person who is short of time and has lost something of value that must be found, Edna tossed out everything the trunk contained. The floor was littered. There were fancy-dress costumes from Grandpa Ferris's era; Christmas hats; bundles of documents; Minnie Mouse shoes; and old photograph albums that flung open their stiff insect-ridden pages when they fell, as though they demanded, after their long burial, to be looked at.

If she could not find anything among this lot, she would be reduced to going down the front steps at three o'clock to meet Peter Westgate in her jeans.

Edna ransacked the pile of stuff. She tried on a Marie Antoinette costume, but it was far too small and the seams split; there was a Robin Hood outfit, but that was too big, and besides it was for a man.

At last something fitted, and it seemed the nearest to being most suitable: a Chinese garment that fell in a trunk of flaking gold from neck to toe. Edna improvised. She tied a broad green sash around her waist, put a sprig of wax holly in her hair and picked up a fan made of pinkish ostrich feathers.

The Chinese dress did not give her feet much room to move in. Edna hobbled to Evadne Ferris's bedroom to inspect herself in the long mirror behind the door.

Her reflection screamed at her, and she knew straight off that she could not go to the Commercial Hotel like this. She felt cornered and on the point of defeat. She sat in a helpless attitude on the edge of the brass bed and wondered if she would begin to cry.

However, before any tears had a chance of springing up, the situation shed its shadows, and she smiled. She saw clearly that whether or not she had anything to wear to the dance did not matter. Because the dance itself did not count. It was true Peter Westgate had asked her to it—but she reminded herself that this was only something on the surface. What he had really asked her was to go away with him.

So Edna took off her strange clothes and threw aside the sprig of holly and the fan; and she put on once again her jeans and khaki shirt.

Then she went to her room and packed all her belongings in a suitcase. They did not amount to much.

She thought it was safe to go and sit on the veranda now and await his arrival.

Passing the grandfather clock, she could not resist a glance at it; and she was staggered to see that the time stood at five minutes past eight. Surely the clock must have stopped? But when she looked at it more closely, she saw the gray greasy pendulum swinging as usual, lazily.

She wanted to fetch an ax and destroy this evidence of the cruelty of time in her life. Instead, Edna did a sum and worked out that she would have to wait six hours and fifty-five minutes before the car drove up. It was a distance in time that dismayed her, but there was no way she could telescope it. She would simply have to sit it out.

Edna picked up a magazine from the stack under the grass table and turned the pages, idly. She had forgotten about the man in the shaving-cream advertisement. All of a sudden, he was in front of her, as though he had come to claim her. She got a jolt. Edna ripped out the page and tore it up. She no longer needed him. In this way she brought an end to her fantasy about the man.

What seemed like three hours later—but was in reality only one—Edna heard her father in the house. She was relieved he was back, but she did not get up and go to him. She now felt shy about thanking him for rescuing her. He would come out in a bit.

However, the sound of his footsteps—they were fast—retreated and died out, and a short while later she heard the truck starting up. Its tires slithered in the mud. He was most likely off to Gowani for brandy and some oblivion. But the truck did not come round the front of the house. Her ears told her it was taking the back track to the west.

Listening for the truck's return gave Edna a distraction. Mr. Ferris was not gone long, for about half an hour. From far off she heard the hooter jabbing at the peace of the day. As the truck drew nearer, its blaring increased, until Edna had to put her hands over her ears. It was stampeding in.

The truck hurtled round the side of the house on two wheels in a spray of mud, and she thought her father must have gone mad. A cluster of fowls gave way hysterically and flew onto the roof.

Too late, Mr. Ferris tried to stop the vehicle. He trod on the brakes. Bottles and baking-powder tins shot into the air. The truck careened off the driveway, slid and lurched across the vacant flower beds, pitched down the bank onto the tennis court, and overturned.

If Mr. Ferris had done this with the intention of frightening Edna, he had succeeded. She raced down the steps.

The wheels spun uselessly in the air and the engine churned and throbbed. "Dad, Dad—are you all right?" she called. "What have you done now?"

Then she heard him laughing, guffawing really, as he sometimes did at Father O'Leary's jokes. His laughter was genuine.

Mr. Ferris dragged himself out of the cab and stood in front of her, and she saw at once that there had been an extraordinary alteration in him, as though, since he had left the house the previous afternoon, a revolution had taken place in him. His body was firm, it seemed, and his shoulders had lost their stoop. If a face can shine from inside, his did at this moment as, looking directly and openly into her eyes, he prodded her and said, "What do you suppose, my girlie? What do you think?"

That something right out of the usual had happened was evident, but there was still the likelihood that he was playing some final grotesque trick on her, a last attempt to trap her, and Edna was cautious. "I haven't the faintest," she said.

Mr. Ferris paused and swallowed and then he flung out his arms as if to embrace the world itself. "I have found it! I have found the fortune!"

Edna could not have been more astonished if the sun had pulled up and turned back in its tracks. She had long ceased to believe in the existence of Grandpa Ferris's sovereigns.

Now, one side of her feared that her father was really deluded; but the other was certain that this time Mr. Ferris could not be lying. The money was far too important a matter for that. There could be no pretense.

Mr. Ferris took Edna by the hand and led her to the back of the truck. Three old milk cans had been pitched out when the truck had turned over and they were embedded in the clay of the tennis court, battered milestones. He prized open the lid of one of them, dipped in a hand, and drew out some coins that were green with mold.

Mr. Ferris thrust them on her, saying in a gabble, "Now you will stay, won't you? Everything has changed since yesterday. You and I will be the richest people in the Territory. People will come visiting Archie Ferris again. We'll have indoor sanitation. You won't leave me, will you?"

Edna's decision was irrevocable.

"You can study to be a radiographer by correspondence course. . . ."

Yesterday, when he had held her and kissed her, had brought her a moment of clarity, and she had been shown the danger and destruction that existed in their relationship.

Her mind was made up. Her life had been launched on a track of its own and there was no point whatsoever in trying to haul her back. How could she convey this to him and convince him?

She was far beyond his reach. Even if he were to offer her a million pounds, she would be waiting at three o'clock for Peter Westgate.

So Edna merely shook her head.

Mr. Ferris did not notice. He was wrought up, in a ferment of excitement, as his hands went in and out of the can, until the sovereigns were a carpet of rust at their feet.

Edna stole a look at his face. The suffering—and she acknowledged that the man had suffered—that had been drawn on it over the years had been rubbed off. His eyes were bright; he looked much younger. She could see the likeness to the man in the rugby team photograph on the dining-room wall.

The finding of Grandpa Ferris's hoard had opened for him a new future of hope and purpose. It had come just in time.

"The diamonds must be somewhere! Father mentioned diamonds."

As Mr. Ferris scrabbled about in the milk can, Edna fell to wondering if he really cared or not whether she stayed now, if he had simply spoken these words as a kind of habit.

This wealth could cure his loneliness. She visualized Evadne Ferris haring back as soon as the news reached her, to stake her claim. He would never again have to grapple with his fear of death as he lay alone in his bed.

At the same time, Edna wondered how much of a blessing the fortune would turn out to be, how much of a change it would bring; whether, in fact, it did not contain pitfalls.

But this was hardly the sort of matter to be considering now. The question that was uppermost in her mind was where he had found the milk cans.

As he scooped up the muddied coins and dropped them back through the mouth of the can, Mr. Ferris gave his account. He said, "Listen, I'll tell you, but you won't believe me. I didn't want to come home. I walked for miles and miles. There was a broken-down hut, must've been the witch's once upon a time. At any rate, I slept there. The sun was up and when I came out of the door, I saw the milk cans staring me in the face. You see, the river had washed away the bank and there they were unearthed, waiting for me, sticking out their heads just at the edge of the water. I came back here as fast as my legs would carry me to get the truck. Oh, it is too lovely. We will celebrate, my girlie!"

"I am very pleased for your sake." There was a blank that Edna wanted filled. "Thank you for pulling me out of the river," she said.

He did not appear to have heard. He was listening only to the dull clink of the coins as he dropped them into the can. But when she repeated what she had said, he answered quickly, almost snappily, "Don't remind me. Never speak about yesterday."

Edna's memory brought out Sister Clothilde's proverb, "Forget what you cannot bear."

"I won't," she said.

From here on, the day assumed the quality of a muddled dream. The day, which had begun without a formula, became even more disordered.

Edna helped Mr. Ferris lug the milk cans one by one to the house. They were heavy and the two of them laughed as they slid about under the weight.

Mr. Ferris emptied them onto the veranda.

The diamonds were in the third can, in a leather pouch at the bottom, each stone wrapped in a wad of paper. There were thirty diamonds in all, and they filled both Mr. Ferris's hands, so large were some of the stones. There was a yellow one that was on fire and a blue one, icy. He kissed them in his hands, and then he placed them back in the pouch and put the pouch in his shirt pocket.

"Who said twenty thousand pounds? There is twice twenty thousand here!"

The contents of the cans made a considerable pile, an anthill. Mr. Ferris sat cross-legged in front of this cone of wealth and scooped his hands through it, letting the coins trickle through his fingers.

He chuckled, he giggled, he tossed back his head and laughed. His delight was a child's. The coins themselves, having been in the earth for so long, were lusterless, but it was as if the gold they were had transferred into his eyes, which glittered. He tugged a handkerchief out of his back pocket, spat on it, and set about polishing one of the sovereigns.

It was at this stage that Edna became aware they were being watched by numerous people. The uncanny bush telegraph had been at work. The Natives from the kraal and others from a radius of miles had converged on the house. Most had come hurrying on foot, but there was a donkey cart and bicycles as well.

The Natives stood back, hugging the bushes, like timid

buck. Their attention was concentrated on what was going on on the veranda, and they were silent, taking in every move. All these inquisitive eyes focused on her father and her made Edna uneasy. She whispered to him, "Do you see them?"

Mr. Ferris left his pyramid of coins and went to the bottom of the veranda steps. He raised his hands and, speaking in their language, said, "The old baas's money has been found!"

A windy murmur followed, and figures began to detach themselves from the background of thorn trees and take a few paces toward the farmhouse. There they stopped. Edna spotted among them the ancient witch with her mantle of monkey skins and, at her side, Oubaas. Near them was Big Mac, alone. She had never seen so many people gathered together on Sherwood Ranch and the sight of them all, a silent wall, was unnerving.

Next Mr. Ferris, his voice stretched and rather shrill, said, "Because of this great and glorious and historic day, everybody will get a present!" At this the mass babbled and some of the women called, "Aai-ee," a sound like a wail.

"Big Mac and you, you, you . . . come here and help me!"

Mr. Ferris and Big Mac and the five diggers got the truck on its wheels and, heaving and pushing, maneuvered it back onto the driveway. Mr. Ferris came puffing onto the stoep and told Edna he was going to Gowani to buy stuff for a celebration and she was to guard the gold while he was away.

Whereas at the start of this freak day, time had dragged so terribly for Edna, the bondage was now over, and the minutes raced by.

She was being swept along to three o'clock.

Though she sat perfectly still in one of the grass chairs, the money at her feet, she felt breathless and giddy.

When the truck had spluttered away, the line of Natives broke up into groups. The piccanins played with their wire toys; and mothers, having unstrapped their babies from their backs, squatted on the wet ground and fed them. The witch was apart, in slats of shade. Cyprian, too, was left alone by the others.

Mr. Ferris returned at two. It hardly seemed he had gone when he was back, though he had been away a number of hours. They heard him hooting continuously from the farm gate, a fanfare that made them all restless and expectant and got them to their feet.

Mr. Ferris had Sixpence with him on the front seat. The truck was loaded with goods: sacks of flour and salt, cartons of tinned food, crates of liquor, bottles of boiled sweets, bolts of material, yellow plastic ducks. He must have spent a hundred, two hundred pounds on tick at Peerbhay Brothers and denuded the shelves.

The Natives, agitated, milled about the truck, while Mr. Ferris and Sixpence, both of them beaming, stood on the back and passed down *bonsellas* into the forest of upturned hands.

Edna remained on the veranda. She felt apart, a stranger, isolated from what was going on.

The gifts were distributed. Everybody got something: the piccanins the ducks, the women material and foodstuffs. The men were given a bottle of brandy each. They ripped off the aluminum tops and stuck the necks in their mouths.

Edna appreciated how inflammable this might turn out to be by evening, but she did not care. There could be pandemonium, a riot, they could go at each other with knives, they could wreck the house, what did it matter? In a little while, she would be away from it all.

Mr. Ferris invited Sixpence and Big Mac and the five diggers to come and drink on the veranda. For them, the privileged ones, there was whisky and soda. Edna moved to the opposite end of the veranda, and they left her alone.

All around, outside and on the stoep, the noise increased. There were shouts and screams and laughter, hectic and frenzied. The donkey brayed and Oubaas scampered across the roof. The ballroom dancers jerked round to their tune. Whenever they stopped, Sixpence wound up the bottle. Every now and then, Mr. Ferris picked up a handful of sovereigns and flung them about him.

Edna shut herself up from all this.

At half past two, she fetched the suitcase from her room. Three o'clock arrived, but no blue-and-white car appeared out of the mogonono bushes.

Mr. Ferris came across to her unsteadily. His vigor had gone; the whisky had brought back his age. "Here's my girlie all alone," he said, "sitting with her suitcase, missing all the fun. Do you really and truly believe he's coming to collect you? Hey—do you? Cat got your tongue?"

A trap door opened underneath Edna and she fell into space.

"Of course he isn't. But never mind, my girlie." He put out a hand to pat her, but she shrank away from him. "Never mind. We'll manage, won't we, you and I, with our thousands?"

"Go away," said Edna.

"Ho-ho, what's this? Such a crosspatch on a wonderful day like this. I know a little girl who has a little curl right in the middle of her forehead, and when she is good she is very, very . . ."

"You're drunk. Go away! Go away! Go away!" The others on the veranda stared at her, and she knew she must have screamed at her father.

"All right, all right," he said, holding up his hands and backing off.

She fell and fell and fell. The dream was a nightmare now. Would life never be finished torturing her? What else did it have in store for her?

In no time at all, the clock in the passage was striking four.

Then Edna took a grip on herself. Of course, there would be an explanation for why he was an hour late. Naturally there would be. If she allowed herself to continue thinking that he was perhaps not coming, she would go mad.

The group at the other end of the veranda was laughing and pointing at her, all except Big Mac, who was asleep, sprawled in a grass chair.

She could not stay any longer. She would go out and meet him.

Edna helped herself to a couple of sovereigns that had rolled her way, and she picked up her suitcase.

"Cheerio!" said Mr. Ferris, merrily. "See you later. It's a long hike to the Capital." Drink made him another person.

"Come on, Archie," said Sixpence, "you mustn't tease her." He was the old Elias; he had taken Elias's place.

At the bottom of the steps, Edna paused to pat the stone lions, both the one with the head and the one without.

The Natives encamped in the garden and on the tennis court—some rowdy, others doped—took no notice of her as she moved off from the house; but Oubaas spotted her and scaled down from the roof and made for her, until the witch called him away.

The last people she passed were the piccanins. They were putting on an act, reeling about, turning somersaults, standing on their hands.

Edna made a detour. She hurried toward the cemetery, the suitcase banging against her.

The plump lizards darted into their holes. The rain had leveled the hump of soil of the newest grave. There was nothing to mark it; nobody could tell that the baby was buried there.

Edna did not linger under the motseara trees. She blew a kiss to the graves of her mother and Grandpa Ferris and went on, skirting the earth dam. Its floor of cracked baked mud had gone. The dam was full of silvery water. Two Egyptian geese and some red-billed ducks bobbed on the tiny waves that knocked against each other. The three stunted willow trees along the catchment bank had sucked up some green.

Beyond the dam, Edna stopped. She opened the suitcase and fished out the ring and put it on her thumb.

She took a footpath through the bush. On the fleshy frond of an aloe, she saw her initials and those of Peter Westgate enclosed in a heart. The scratches were fainter because they had begun to heal.

After a while, she reached the road. She walked fast, jumping over the yellow puddles, her bare feet crunching the mud that was drying out. Soon the noise of the party at the house grew fainter and fainter, and she was in silence. There were two pied crows on top of a euphorbia tree and in a corner of her vision a Marico sunbird flashed. Her eyes searched for a third crow so as to avoid bad luck.

The road was covered with mud pimples, little mounds pushed up by earthworms. Flying ants thrust themselves from holes in a continual pressing stream and tried out their wings. They crashed softly into Edna, and she brushed them off her face with her free hand.

She threaded her way along the tunnel through the mogonono bushes.

After about ten minutes, Edna became conscious that she was being followed. When she stopped, whoever it was behind her stopped as well.

At length Edna swung round and she caught the albino before he had a chance to dive off the road. He was about thirty yards behind her, and she noticed in his one hand a yellow duck and in the other the Teddy bear. "Good-bye, Cyprian. I am going away," Edna called. "You mustn't follow me any more, please."

He dropped the toy duck and returned her wave, and she went on alone.

All this while Edna listened for the sound of the car, but there was only the twittering and screeching of birds and, once, the snort of an impala.

Every bend she took she expected to see the car in front of her, but the track remained empty.

At length she reached the main road and she passed through the stone gateway and crossed to the farm stall.

There she sat on a boulder and faced north.

She had not been in this position long when a voice said, giving her goose flesh, "Miss Ferris? Is that you, Miss Ferris?" Edna swiveled round and she made out clearly, between the planks of the stall, two gray eyes staring at her. One of them was squint, so she spat through her fingers.

Edna had to coax Brother Martin out.

At last she succeeded, taking him by the hand, telling him he was safe with her, he could trust her. He came out shyly, blinking. And his lips gave their queer jerky smile. He said, "I ran away again." The red of his cheeks spread into the rest of his face.

"Don't be ashamed," said Edna. "There's nothing to be ashamed about. Where are you going? To your sister's in Durban again?"

Brother Martin's right eyebrow crept up. He shook his head. "No. It didn't work. It wasn't God's will. But I learned something: I found out that I don't really mean to run away, deep down inside me. I just want to get out of the place for a bit, and then I'm better. I'll go back to the Mission now and Sister Clothilde will be all smiles."

Once, in the "Palace," he had told her that his God had deserted him. She was not equipped to question him about this. "I understand," said Edna. "At least I think I do. Well," she continued, shifting off this ground, "if you like, I'll ask my friend to give you a lift, so you needn't walk. He's been a bit delayed but he'll be arriving any minute. You may have wondered what I'm doing here. As a matter of fact, I am going away. It is God's will. Please tell Sister Clothilde and tell her I'll write."

"Is his name Peter?" said Brother Martin.

"How did you know?" asked Edna, alarmed.

The jumpy smile was back on him. "I read the message on the door."

Edna laughed. "Oh look," she said, "there's a ladybird on you." She plucked the insect off the sleeve of his shirt.

"Ladybird, ladybird, fly away home,
Your house is on fire, and your children all gone."

Edna blew on the ladybird and it sailed off her hand.

The sun was going down and the shadows were denser. The water tanks at Gowani Siding caught the dying rays and blazed for a minute, then went out. A blanket was spread over the clumps of karree trees there, smothering their greenness.

A lost cow ambled down the white road and stopped to scratch its chin on a telephone pole.

The sound reached her before it did him, and her heart went into her mouth. "What's that?" They both listened.

Then Brother Martin pointed to the east, high in the sky, where there was a dot.

The Davidsons were coming.

The plane grew in size as it descended, racing to beat the night, and the din of its engine increased. Before long it passed low over them, and Edna and Brother Martin flattened themselves against the wall of the farm stall. The cow charged into the bush.

The plane skimmed into the rim of the sun, a black moth.

In a minute or so it had landed and the hush of the veld came back.

"For a second, I thought it was him," said Edna. "It's funny, I'd forgotten all about those people. I suppose they're still trying to sell the place."

Brother Martin looked at his feet. He said, haltingly, "We had our own little world there, didn't we?"

Edna was saddened. "I'll never forget that," she said, and the words seemed inadequate to her. "No, I'll never."

They walked to the boulder and sat there. Makagabe Hill was in front of them. The spoonbill storks, late, flapped through the air. There was a bond between Edna and Brother Martin. They sat, exchanging few words.

The cow reappeared. A host of green and white rain butterflies, their life at its close, floated down the road. That was the last touch of color of the day, except for the short flare of purple and red as the sun fell behind the horizon.

The twilight, with its scudding squeaking bats, was over quickly, too. They heard a jackal howling and, close at hand, a small animal squealed as an owl snapped it up.

There was no traffic on the road, either up or down.

They sat, the two of them, on the boulder. After a long, long while, Edna said in a taut voice, "What's the time, please?"

The day had hauled her through so many moods, lifting her up and casting her down, battering her, exhilarating her, confusing her, that by now her emotions were on the point of exhaustion.

She was faced finally with despair; she could not run away from it.

Brother Martin struck a match. "A few minutes after nine," he said. "Not quite five past." The match went out.

Six hours since three o'clock . . .

As a defense against being engulfed by hopelessness, Edna let the tears spill down her cheeks.

Awkwardly, Brother Martin put an arm round her shoulders. His two-day beard prickled her skin. "Please don't cry," he said, his breath milky on her. "We can't always be unhappy."

She clung to him desperately and sobbed into his shirt, "What will I do? What will I do if he doesn't come?" She was at rock bottom.

Brother Martin drew his face away from hers. "I'll tell you what," he said, doubtfully, unsure of himself. He coughed. "I have a plan, a good idea." It was as though he had himself to convince as well as Edna. "If," he continued, gaining confidence, "if your friend doesn't come to fetch you, I won't go back to the Mission. There you are. You and I will go away together. That's what."

The words were loose in her head and did not make an impression at first. But once she had assembled them and it came to her what he had offered to do, her tears were stopped, and she gasped. She knew that life, at its lowest, had presented her with a moment so precious that it would remain with her, shining bright, to the last of her days.

Edna smiled in the darkness. "I don't know what to say." She was truly at a loss. "Except . . . Except . . ." The words were stuck. She grasped others. "I want to give you something."

She was feeling in her back pocket for one of the sovereigns —a keepsake; she had thought for an instant of giving him the ring, but no—when, "Look," said Brother Martin. "Look over there."

She followed his finger. The road was a pale white ribbon in the starlight.

She screwed up her eyes. There was a change. Suddenly, it was as if the moon had begun to rise in the wrong place. A glow gradually outlined the ridge of Makagabe Hill, gently, then starkly.

The light grew stronger. And then they heard the car.

Soon it reached the top of the rise and two head lamps splashed orange onto the road.

"It's him!" cried Edna, rushing into the road. "It's him!" She waved her arms, jumping up and down. Her eyes were dazzled. She was a springhare trapped in the beams. In her head a colossal orchestra played the "Toreador Song," drowning the sound of the car, bursting her ears.

The car swooped down on her, a brilliant night bird.

There was a smell of rubber burning and then the lights that had blinded her went out. The music ceased and a car door banged. She groped in the dark.

The next moment she was in his arms, trembling so much that she felt she might fall to pieces.

"God, what a business," said Peter Westgate. "The big river was in flood and the police wouldn't let us cross until an hour ago."

She didn't hear him.

Other cars came now, those that had also been held up, a procession of lamps down the incline of the hill.

Peter Westgate moved Edna to the side of the road. "I'm so sorry," he kept repeating.

The oncoming cars made a strip of light in the night. The stone lions guarding the gateway glowed on top of their pillars.

"You came!" said Edna. "You came!"

Some of the cars hooted a greeting.

After a short while, the convoy had gone past on its way to the south, and they were back in darkness. She rested her head against him; she was very tired. He stroked her hair, stilling her trembling. He kissed her.

Edna said, "We'll be terribly late for the dance, you know."

"The dance doesn't matter."

"It doesn't?"

Her gamble had paid off. She had won! Edna was aware that she would never be able to calculate accurately the relief his words had brought her.

"No, it doesn't."

Edna looked up into the blurred stars, as if there was a place in the sky she was about to fill.

"I'll explain to you as we go," said Peter Westgate. "We have a lot to tell each other. Come." He led her to the car and opened the door. A light clicked on, showing up the blue interior. When she stepped inside, she would be entering, at last, her new world. Sherwood Ranch would be forsaken forever. Her moment had come.

Then she remembered Brother Martin. "Oh," said Edna. "There's a friend of mine somewhere about and I wonder if we could give him a lift. Only as far as the Mission."

Nothing surprised Peter Westgate. "Surely."

"Brother Martin!" Edna called. "We're ready to go now." She waited until her words had faded in the air. She stepped back from the car. "Brother Martin, where are you? Come along, now. Don't be scared."

But there was no reply. Brother Martin had slipped away and disappeared into the veld.

"Well, here *I* am, at any rate," said Edna.

DATE DUE

GAYLORD			PRINTED IN U.S.A.